"Do you make follow-up visits to everyone you send away, or only those you get falsely convicted?"

The injustice of it all flared up. Susannah still raged inside at the flagrant *wrongness* of the verdict.

"I'm trying to determine if we had all the facts eight years ago," Jared hedged.

"I thought you were as sure as God about who killed Timothy Winters. Your partner was."

Jared held her gaze for a long moment.

Susannah wished she knew what he was thinking. Why look into a case eight years old? One, moreover, that should have been stamped solved?

"Three days ago someone told me a friend of theirs had seen Timothy Winters alive and well in San Francisco."

Susannah stared at him, almost afraid to believe her ears. Her heart skipped a beat. The room faded from view as she stared at the man who sat so arrogantly across from her.

Timothy was alive?

Dear Reader,

We've all heard it said that love conquers all. But does it really? What if everything you hold dear is taken from you—your home, job, freedom, even your baby. And then years later you are given a second chance—with the very person who was instrumental in taking everything away. When most people are establishing new careers, getting a first home or starting a family, Susannah was stuck in prison for a crime she didn't commit.

Could love overcome such odds?

That's what Susannah has to find out when she gets out of prison and the only person to help is the assistant district attorney who prosecuted her. The man who is consumed with guilt for his part in convicting an innocent woman. Now he's out to right all wrongs. Is falling in love part of the equation, or is it only remorse and a desire for restitution?

I always wondered how much love could overcome. Join me and see the healing power of true love.

Please feel free to visit my Web site at www.barbaramcmahon.com!

All the best,

Barbara McMahon

The First Day
Barbara McMahon

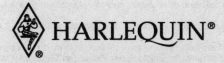

HARLEQUIN®

TORONTO • NEW YORK • LONDON
AMSTERDAM • PARIS • SYDNEY • HAMBURG
STOCKHOLM • ATHENS • TOKYO • MILAN • MADRID
PRAGUE • WARSAW • BUDAPEST • AUCKLAND

ISBN 0-373-71235-9

THE FIRST DAY

Copyright © 2004 by Barbara McMahon.

To Sheila Slattery, who always believed in Susannah.
May your move to Oregon be happy.
Live long and prosper, my friend.

Books by Barbara McMahon

HARLEQUIN SUPERROMANCE
1179—THE RANCHER'S BRIDE

HARLEQUIN ROMANCE
3649—TEMPORARY FATHER
3657—THE HUSBAND CAMPAIGN
3669—THE MARRIAGE TEST
3686—THE SUBSTITUTE WIFE
3698—HIS SECRETARY'S SECRET
3734—THE SHEIKH'S PROPOSAL
3753—THE TYCOON PRINCE
3785—THE BOSS'S CONVENIENT PROPOSAL

Don't miss any of our special offers. Write to us at the
following address for information on our newest releases.

Harlequin Reader Service
U.S.: 3010 Walden Ave., P.O. Box 1325, Buffalo, NY 14269
Canadian: P.O. Box 609, Fort Erie, Ont. L2A 5X3

PROLOGUE

OH, GOD, please let this nightmare end! Susannah Chapman prayed, her heart pounding wildly, her palms clammy. Her stomach churned. She couldn't breathe. For a moment she feared she would faint. Surely everyone in the courtroom could hear the blood pounding through her veins, could feel the overwhelming fear that filled every cell of her body. How could this have gone so far?

She stared straight ahead at the walnut paneling on the front of the judge's bench. Tuning out the sounds of the courtroom, the sounds that had grown more and more familiar as each day had progressed, she tried to hold on to her control.

She was so scared. Never in her wildest dreams had she imagined things going so wrong. The American legal system was built to defend justice, not make a mockery of it. How could twelve men and women find her guilty of a crime she had not committed?

She swayed slightly.

The nightmare was endless. Sliding her hands beneath the edge of the table, she pinched one thumb, trying to wake up. The pain was sharp and sudden.

But she was still in the courtroom awaiting the judge's sentence.

Swallowing against the rising bile that threatened to spew out, she took a shaky breath. She'd felt sick for weeks, unable to eat, unable to concentrate, fighting the injustice of the situation with all she had. Which, granted, wasn't much.

The jury was seated in the box. Present to hear the sentence their guilty verdict demanded.

From the corner of her eye she saw the young deputy district attorney lounging carelessly in his chair, talking with someone she couldn't see without turning her head. The prosecuting D.A. sat upright, smug, radiating triumph. Why wouldn't they believe her? Timothy Winters had been alive the last time she saw him.

Focusing ahead, she took another breath. She rubbed her palms surreptitiously on her skirt, trying to dry the dampness, trying to quell the fearful dread. She dropped her gaze to the table before her. Harry Lind, her attorney, had file folders neatly before him.

"Are you all right?" he asked before a paroxysm of coughing took over. He'd been ill during the entire travesty of a trial. But he had pushed onward, her only hope.

She shook her head slightly. "I think I'm going to throw up," she whispered back.

"Hang in there. It will all be over soon." His tone sounded bracing, but Susannah wasn't reassured. The trial might be over soon, but the nightmare would go on forever.

She looked directly at the opposing counsel. He had been relentless in his prosecution. Especially when she'd taken the stand. She had tried to convince him she had done nothing wrong, but he hammered at her until she became confused and she knew her testimony sounded muddled. She was no match for a district attorney with years of experience behind him. Especially one up for reelection and anxious to get a quick conviction to clinch the vote.

He had gone after her as though he had a personal vendetta against her. She had hoped the cross-examination by her own attorney would have minimized the damage for the jury. It hadn't. Now her only hope lay in an appeal.

The judge arrived, taking his place behind the bench.

Blinking back tears of frustration and anger, Susannah stared straight ahead again as the judge rapped his gavel.

She wiped her hands against her skirt again and stared at the man, her heart in her throat.

''We have to stand, now,'' Harry said, his hand coming beneath her arm to assist her up.

Susannah stood, her legs feeling wobbly. Turning slightly she stared at the men and women on the jury. They were strangers. They didn't know her. They hadn't known Shawn, or Timothy. The evidence had been skewed. From that alone they shouldn't have had the power to decide her fate. They didn't *know* her!

"…found the defendant, Susannah Chapman, guilty of murder in the first degree…"

She swayed, steadied by her attorney, his hand her only anchor. She stared as if through a fog. The nausea gained a stronger grip. She held her breath hoping she wouldn't vomit all over the shiny table before her. It was the only trace of pride she could muster.

"…life in prison, without parole," the judge droned.

Susannah had a manic desire to laugh. She had come to Denver to begin a career, get married and start a family. She was only twenty-one years old. She had her whole life before her.

She swallowed hard, fear and terror gaining a foothold. She had her whole life before her but she needn't worry about establishing a career. Needn't worry about going it alone after Shawn's death. The state of Colorado had decided her future for her.

She was to spend the rest of her life in prison for a crime she hadn't committed.

"We'll appeal," Harry said gruffly, coughing into his handkerchief again.

Susannah looked at him as if he were a stranger.

Glancing over to the prosecutor, she stared at him, fear clawing at her, nausea threatening to overcome her control, anger churning. His triumphant satisfaction grated. He was surrounded by men and women congratulating him. Smiling, laughing, slapping him on the back as if he'd just accomplished some great feat. Not as if he had ruined her life.

The press strained across the wooden railing that separated the spectators from the participants in the courtroom drama, vying for attention, calling out questions, cameras flashing.

For a moment the tall, dark-haired assistant district attorney turned and his gaze locked with hers. His eyes held a trace of compassion. Susannah stared at him, willing him to do something.

"I didn't do it," she whispered. Somehow she had to get it across to him. He had to believe her. Someone had to!

"Let's go, miss." A marshal was at her side, the cold, steel handcuffs snapping sharply over her wrists.

Turning, Susannah took two steps and slid into a faint.

CHAPTER ONE

"MRS. WALKER is here to see you," Rose said when Jared Walker picked up his phone.

"Send her in." He replaced the receiver and stood, almost glad to take a break, but wishing it were someone else, anyone else, interrupting. He'd been reading a deposition taken by one of his assistants and still had a slew of questions he needed answered. They'd have to call the man back in. Dammit, he hated inefficiency.

"Hello, love." Noelle stood in the doorway for a moment, poised for an entrance.

"Hello, Noelle. What brings you by? Is Eric all right?"

She hadn't changed a bit, had always been dramatic. For a moment, he tried to remember what it had been like to be so passionately caught up in her spell he couldn't think straight. That had ended long ago. Now he wondered where his head had been.

He came around the desk and waited for her to reach up and kiss his cheek which she did every time they met. He knew the routine, and would not make an issue of it. Their relationship had formally ended eighteen months ago. Now, she was merely the mother of his son. She tried to make more of it, but he wasn't interested. That fire and passion had evaporated long ago.

"He's fine. He loves kindergarten. Why, I can't imagine. I didn't like school at all, except for the extracurricular activities and the dances," she said, looking around the cluttered office.

"He's a little young for dances," Jared said dryly. He waited until she sat in one of the visitor chairs facing his desk, carefully crossing her legs to give him the maximum view. So typically Noelle. Ignoring her blatant sexuality, he dropped into the matching chair beside hers.

She often stopped by the office—especially since the divorce. Usually she tried to interest him in escorting her to some charity event, though recently she'd begun to see a man named Martin.

Jared didn't think Noelle needed an escort. Why had she come?

"If he's fine, why are you here?" he asked.

"Darling, can't I stop by just to visit?"

"You've stopped by more lately than when we were married. I'm busy, Noelle. If this is a pleasure call, maybe we should wait until the next time I come to pick up Eric." Not that Jared ever spent a moment with Noelle if he could help it. His time with his son was special, he didn't want to share it with his ex-wife, who still seemed to cling to the hope he'd fall madly in love with her again and take up where they left off.

She studied him, as if trying to gauge his mood.

"Martin is going to London at the end of the week," she said, "and there's a party I want to attend. I would appreciate your escort."

Jared leaned back in his chair, warily watching her. She never gave up. How clear could he make it? They were divorced. He had wanted out of the marriage when the love he'd felt had faded. He was not interested in rekindling old flames. The only regret he had was not having his son live with him.

He missed Eric more than he had expected. At the time, he had believed his young son would be better off with his mother, but now he wished he'd sued for joint custody. How receptive would Noelle be to change? Not at all, if he read things correctly. Rather, she'd try to use that as a negotiating tool to have him come back.

"Go with me," Noelle urged. "It'll do you good to get out and mingle again. All you do is work."

It was an old argument. His devotion to work had been her most common complaint when they'd been married.

"Besides, you miss all the gossip going around," she said. "Do you remember the Burroughs, Don and Fran? They're friends of my parents."

Jared nodded. "I remember meeting them. Don't they always go to the New Year's Day function your folks put on?"

"Usually. I ran into them the other afternoon, and they had the most outlandish tale you can imagine."

He waited. Obviously she had something to say. Used to her tricks, he kept silent. Noelle liked being coaxed, but that could take all afternoon. If he appeared disinterested, she'd get to the point faster. And he could get back to work that much sooner.

"Honestly, Jared, aren't you the least curious?"

"About what friends of your parents had to say to you? Not really."

She shrugged. "It was nonsense. They claim they saw Timothy in San Francisco two weeks ago."

"What? That's impossible. He's been dead for eight years," he said evenly. For an instant that courtroom scene flashed into his mind. The young woman convicted of the crime had been scared silly. He could still see the fear and anger in her eyes, hear her protestations of innocence.

It had been his first murder conviction after joining the district attorney's office. Graduating at the top of his class, he had bypassed the get-rich-quick aspects of defense law, choosing to pursue justice with the prosecution. He'd been so young, so eager, so enthusiastic.

He'd thought he had the world by the tail after that conviction. Michael Denning had been the district attorney, and the high-profile murder of a son of one of Denver's leading families had given him the flurry of attention needed at the last moment to assure his reelection.

The conviction had also assured Jared's alliance with Noelle Winters. Denver's leading family had been more than eager to welcome him after that, despite his background.

She shrugged. "They saw him. See what you miss by not going to parties?"

"It was someone who looks like him," Jared said. "Noelle, he's dead. His body was identified by his father."

"With his face blown away? I always wondered how my uncle could have recognized him at all." She hesitated. "They seemed sure it was Timothy."

"Did they speak to him? Find out what the hell he's doing in San Francisco when we all thought him dead and buried here in Denver? Did they find out why he hadn't contacted his family in all this time? It's a double, Noelle."

"Of course, I know that. They didn't speak to him, just saw him. But when they approached him, he turned, spotted them and then ran into an office building. What if it were Timothy?"

"Impossible!" He rose and strode to the window. His office was on the twelfth floor. His view looked west, to the Front Range of the Rockies. Snow already blanketed the peaks of the distant mountains, the closer peaks too low to have snow this early in October. Usually the view calmed him, gave him a sense of freedom he relished.

Today, however, he didn't even see the view. If what Noelle suggested was remotely possible, it was a prosecutor's worst nightmare—the conviction of an innocent person.

"Let me know if you change your mind about the party. Otherwise I'll have to go alone and I hate driving home that late by myself."

"I won't change my mind," he said. He turned to face her, struck again by her sleek good looks. Her auburn hair was feathered and curled around her face, softening the angles and planes. The sophisticated style suited her. Her clothes spoke of elegance and expense. Her makeup was discreet, though she had little need for any. She was a stunning woman.

But to him at this moment, it was as if she were a stranger. He knew she'd never been fully in love with him. He'd often wondered why she'd married him. For excitement? He had not lived up to her expectations, wishing to work more than party. But she hadn't liked it when he'd called it quits. When was she going to believe they were through? If it weren't for Eric, he wouldn't voluntarily see her again.

He had his work. And on weekends, his son came to stay with him. Jared would petition to change the custody agreement as Eric grew older. He wanted to spend more time than just weekends with Eric.

"Well, if you won't, you won't." She rose. "Would you like to have dinner next week? Eric would love to see you midweek."

The one pull he couldn't resist.

"Dinner only, Noelle," he warned. "Did the Burroughs say anything else?"

She shrugged. "It was just party conversation. I'll

ask them if you want. But as you say, Timothy is buried here in Denver.''

Jared stared at the closed door after she'd gone, his mind considering the ramifications of the startling announcement she'd made.

It couldn't be true.

He closed his eyes, seeing images from that trial as clearly as if it had been yesterday. The gun found at Susannah Chapman's apartment building hidden in the thick clump of bushes near the garage. The blood splatter on the barrel. The identification of the corpse by Noelle's uncle, Gerald Winters. The rush with which Michael had pushed through the case, schmoozing with the reporters every chance he got in his effort to get reelected.

Opening his eyes, Jared crossed to the desk. Dialing his secretary, Rose, he waited impatiently for her to respond.

''Get me the files on the Timothy Winters murder case. It was eight years ago.''

''Was it resolved?'' Rose asked.

''We got a conviction.'' The possibility of Timothy being alive was disquieting. If he were, who had the dead man been? Had Susannah Chapman killed him? The motive had been heavily weighted on her killing Timothy as revenge for his causing the death of her fiancé. She had no reason he knew of to kill anyone but Timothy.

Had he been instrumental in sending an innocent woman to prison?

His soul chilled.

He couldn't believe that. He'd done his job. It had been an important, high-profile case. Michael had been the lead prosecutor and had been ruthless in his pursuit. But he'd followed procedures. He wouldn't have gone for a conviction if everything hadn't pointed to her guilt, no matter what the polls showed.

"The files will probably be in the archives. It could take a couple of days to have them sent," Rose said.

"Get them today," he snapped.

Taking a deep breath, Jared tried to figure out what to do if Timothy was alive and living in San Francisco. Who had been killed?

One step at a time—he'd review the court transcripts. See if there was any possibility of error. If so, he would look into it further. Otherwise, he'd chalk it up to the Burroughs seeing Timothy's doppelganger.

He'd hold off telling his boss anything until he knew more. Steve Johnson loved being district attorney as much as Michael had eight years ago. He'd been appointed after Michael had died suddenly of a heart attack two years into his term. Four years ago, Steve had won easily. For the most part, Johnson had done a credible job. There were one or two incidents they'd had to hush up. But Jared knew Steve planned to use the position as a stepping stone for bigger things. Politically savvy, Steve could rationalize waiting to investigate until after the election, only four weeks away.

Jared ran his fingers through his hair. He needed to review the files, to see if there was anything to even suggest that every avenue had not been explored, every aspect of the crime hadn't been examined. Had they overlooked something?

The image of young Susannah Chapman rose. She'd been slender, with long blond hair and big blue eyes. Pretty in a quiet way. He remembered her stricken features, the confusion that played across her face as if she couldn't believe how the trial had progressed.

It had been his first murder case and the pressure before the election had been tremendous. He had been courting Noelle at the time and had wanted to win at any cost, to impress her, her father, her entire family. The evidence had been circumstantial for the most part, but with the motive and the video footage of her threatening Timothy that the news team had captured at Shawn Anderson's funeral, it had proved strong enough for a conviction.

He sat down and pulled the phone closer. In seconds he had the number for the Burroughs.

Twenty minutes later he called the San Francisco Police Department.

CHAPTER TWO

THE SUN FELT GOOD on Susannah's back as she attacked the ground with the hoe. She had shed her jacket earlier, the October sunshine warm enough to keep the coolness of the breeze from chilling. Her muscles strained against the rich, fragrant soil. She wiped her forehead with the back of her wrist and took another breath of the clean mountain air. All too soon the weather would turn colder and her assignments would be confined to indoor chores. The vegetable garden would be put on hold for several months, until spring planting.

She hated being inside. She felt more confined, more imprisoned when she didn't get to work out of doors. It was all she could do sometimes to keep from screaming until she completely lost her mind.

The crush of women milling around, talking, shoving, laughing, increased her feeling of suffocation. By March she would become panic-stricken just entering the mess hall. She'd have to force herself to breathe when she was locked in her cell. The confined space was the worst part of incarceration. She could stand the way of life, if she didn't battle claustrophobia every waking moment.

Fortunately each year she was reassigned to the garden task force and could escape to the outdoors for hours every day. It was all that kept her sane.

She dug deep into the dark soil, turning it for the last time before winter, wondering what they would grow next year. Her zucchini had been the largest ever this past year. She secretly thought the extra fertilization had helped, but hadn't told the guards she had added more than the recommended amount. Let them think what they would about the crop, she knew more than they did about growing things. Cared more than they did.

"Chapman."

Susannah looked up, took an involuntary step backward as the correctional officer loomed over her. Tasting the apprehension that rose being near large, muscular men, she took a deep breath and tried to control her features to make sure he had no idea of the fear that roiled within. She had that mastered after all this time even though the fear itself never fully went away.

"Yes?"

"Warden wants to see you."

She blinked in surprise. She hadn't seen the warden since that time five years ago when—

"Now!"

She looked at the hoe in bewilderment. This had never happened before, what was she supposed to do?

"Do I turn in the tools or will I be coming back?" she asked.

"Don't know. Leave them. You'll probably be back. I haven't heard otherwise."

Laying down the hoe, she snatched her jacket up from the ground and carried it over her arm. She walked beside the officer, trying to keep as much distance between them as she could without it becoming obvious. She didn't need any trouble with him. Or any of the guards. Thankfully most of them were women, not that they were any more sympathetic to the inmates.

It was a long way to the administration section from the garden and every step of the way Susannah wondered why she had been summoned. Except for the time she'd been beaten by that guard out to whip all the inmates into shape, as he'd put it, she had never seen the warden on a one-on-one basis.

Had she done something wrong? Thinking about the past few days, she could come up with nothing. She did her work, kept to herself. Her only friend was Marissa and she was clean. Due to be released in a few months, Marissa was not going to jeopardize that.

Susannah sighed softly, the sadness tugging at her heart whenever she thought about her friend leaving. She would have no one then. Yet she didn't begrudge Marissa her freedom. The woman had saved her sanity. She would never have been able to survive this long if it hadn't been for Marissa's advice. Susannah would miss her as much as she missed Shawn, as she missed—

No, she couldn't think about that. That was one

thing Marissa had taught her—don't think about
things that became too painful. There was no release,
no outlet, so no use in thinking about it.

She hoped the meeting with the warden didn't take
too long. She wanted to get back to work, to stay in
the late-autumn sun as long as she could. All too soon
she would be transferred inside and have to cope with
the confining aspects of winter that were so hard to
endure.

WARDEN GILLIAN GRIFFIN sat behind her desk and
studied Jared Walker. He returned her gaze, wondering how long it would take for Susannah Chapman to
arrive.

"We didn't expect you," the warden said, rear-
ranging some papers on her desk.

"It was a spur-of-the-moment decision to come."
And probably a dumb move, to boot. But Jared hadn't
been able to resist.

He leaned back in the visitor's chair and mustered
as much patience as he could. He had no intention of
explaining anything at this point. He needed to talk
to Susannah first. Needed a few more facts.

"Chapman's not aware that you are her visitor. I
only requested that she join us."

"Do you have an interrogation room where we
could meet privately?" he asked.

She smiled. "We are not a police department, Mr.
Walker. We have no interrogation rooms, just visitor

centers. You and inmate Chapman can use one of those if you feel my office is inappropriate.''

"Not inappropriate, but I don't want to disrupt your own schedule,'' he said smoothly. Nor give anyone a hint of where his inquiries might lead. He still hoped he was wrong. He hoped Chapman would convince him justice had been served eight years ago and let him get back to his present cases.

She smiled again. "How thoughtful of you. Once she arrives, I'll escort you both to a visitor's room close by.''

Jared nodded. He was probably wasting his time. Yet he couldn't dismiss the remote possibility that Timothy Winters might still be alive.

The San Francisco police had not located the man the Burroughs had seen. They had checked Department of Motor Vehicle records, voting records and their own arrest records. No Timothy Winters was listed.

Yet the police had located a firm where a man answering Timothy's description had worked until two weeks prior. When they'd shown the manager the photograph Jared had faxed, he'd been positively identified as John Wiley. Prints from his workstation were being sent to Denver. The San Francisco police were now looking for John Wiley.

That, and the appalling mess of shoddy work he'd discovered in the old files, raised enough doubt in Jared's mind to bring him here.

He had been convinced eight years ago that Susannah Chapman had coldly killed Timothy Winters as revenge for Timothy causing the death of her fiancé, Shawn Anderson. Now he wasn't sure.

The news from San Francisco, plus the mess he'd found in the files, was disturbing. John Wiley had not been seen since the day the Burroughs had spotted him. And the positive photo identification strongly suggested Timothy Winters was alive.

"I must admit to being somewhat curious why one of Denver's leading assistant district attorneys is coming to see an inmate who has not had a visitor during the entire time she's been here," the warden said.

Jared's eyes narrowed. "No visitors?"

"None. Nor any phone calls or letters. Susannah Chapman is alone in the world as I understand it."

"Her fiancé was killed just a couple of weeks before she killed Timothy Winters. Her parents were already dead."

"If she killed Winters," the warden said mildly.

"You doubt it?" he asked sharply. Did she know something he didn't?

Warden Griffin shrugged. "She's maintained she is innocent from the first, which made it especially hard with the baby. She has been a model prisoner, if there is such a thing. Never gives any trouble. She's quiet, well behaved and has only one friend inside. And apparently no friends on the outside."

Jared stared at her. He focused on one word. "Baby?"

The warden raised her eyebrows. "She was pregnant when she arrived here. She had a baby six months later. Gave it up for adoption, of course. She's never going to leave here, why hold up her child's life or create turmoil by placing the child in the foster-care system?''

''I didn't know she was pregnant,'' Jared said. Nothing in the notes or transcripts indicated that fact. Granted the entire proceedings had been rushed. When an unexpected opening became available on the court calendar, Michael had pushed to get the trial scheduled. He'd wanted that conviction prior to the election.

How could her attorney not have played that card? With the changing hormones and everything else attributed to pregnancy, added to the grief at the death of her child's father, he might have gotten her off with manslaughter.

''I don't think she knew herself until after she arrived here,'' the warden explained. ''The whole thing took such a short time, from the death of her fiancé until her conviction. She had other things on her mind.''

At the sound of a knock on the door, the warden crossed the room to open it.

''Come in,'' she said, opening the door wide. To the correctional officer, she nodded. ''Wait a moment, we'll be going to another room.''

Jared watched as Susannah entered the office, swinging wide around the warden, her eyes focused on the woman. He was stunned at the sight of her. Gone was the pretty young woman he remembered from the trial. Gone was the long blond hair, the rosy cheeks, the trim figure. In her place stood a wraith of a woman, so thin she reminded him of pictures he'd seen of concentration-camp victims. Her hair cropped short, almost shorter than his, was still blond and capped her head like a bowl. Her cheekbones showed prominently above the hollows. But it was the wary and hostile expression in her eyes that captured his attention. She'd aged and hardened since he'd last seen her. He should have expected it after eight years in prison, but he hadn't. He'd expected to see the same young woman with the long blond hair.

"I believe you know Mr. Walker?" Warden Griffin said to Susannah.

Susannah turned and froze. Her eyes wide, she stared at him and Jared could almost feel the waves of hostility. Could he blame her? He was one of the men who had built a case against her that had caused her to forfeit her freedom before she had even started in life. He tried to remember twelve men and women had rendered the verdict. But he felt responsible. Was this what happened to all the people he prosecuted?

She nodded, wariness cloaking her like a shield.

"Ms. Chapman."

"Mr. Walker drove down from Denver this morning to speak with you. He can talk to you in one of the visitor's rooms. Follow me." The warden turned and led the way.

Susannah followed without saying a word, the guard falling in beside her.

A model prisoner, the warden had told him. He followed, wondering what she was thinking. Would she cooperate?

Warden Griffin stopped by the open door of a visitor's room. The walls facing the corridor were glass, the far wall had a security window that overlooked the parking lot. She gestured for Susannah to enter, then turned to Jared.

Holding out her hand, she smiled. "If you wish to see me after the interview, feel free to come back. If not, I wish you a pleasant drive home."

"Thank you." He shook her hand, then stepped into the room. The door closed behind him. The guard stationed himself across the hallway, leaning against the wall where he could watch the proceedings, but hear nothing.

SUSANNAH MOVED around the large table and turned to face her foe. She studied him for a long moment, flashbacks to the courtroom overlaying his features. It had been the most awful time of her life, until prison.

He'd stood up well to the wear of time. He looked broader, robust, fit and trim. There was an assurance that had been lacking eight years ago. She expected he was now the lead prosecutor on major cases, not a very junior one.

"Would you care to sit down?" he asked, gesturing to one of the chairs.

Susannah sat gingerly, laying her jacket on the

chair next to her. "What do you want?" she asked as he pulled out a chair across from her and dropped into it.

Putting his briefcase on the table, Jared snapped it open and withdrew a thick file. Susannah watched him warily. Why had he come?

"I wanted to talk to you about the murder of Timothy Winters," he said deliberately.

"Timothy was alive the last time I saw him," she replied, her voice firm, her expression hostile. "But as I recall, you didn't believe me eight years ago. So why should you believe me now?"

"Ms. Chapman, eight years ago last September a man was murdered in Timothy Winters's house by a shotgun blast to the face. Gerald Winters identified the body as his son Timothy. No one else lived in the house. No one else of a similar description was reported missing. Since that night, no one has seen or heard from Timothy Winters. Not his family, not any friends. His bank account was never accessed. Everyone believes he is dead. There has been nothing to suggest otherwise."

She glared at him, but remained silent. She'd heard this at the trial.

"Do you have any reason to suspect Timothy left Denver? Any reason why he wouldn't contact his family, wouldn't use his social security card to get a job?" Jared asked.

Slowly she shook her head. "I only know he came by that night, distraught and asking me to forgive him for causing Shawn's death. It had been an accident. I knew that. But if he hadn't been drinking, it never would have happened. I knew nothing about a shotgun in the bushes behind the apartment. I knew nothing about a dead man. Timothy walked out of my apartment alive and healthy.''

''Never to be seen again?'' Jared said sarcastically.

''I told you what happened eight years ago. I tried to tell everyone when I testified, but your partner twisted everything up.''

''Don't you eat?'' he blurted out, frowning as he looked at her.

Bewilderment crossed her face. ''I eat,'' she said.

''Not enough. You're nothing but skin and bones. A good wind would blow you away.''

Her eyes shimmered in sudden anger. ''Would it matter? What do I have to live for? Another fifty years or so in prison? I would just as soon be dead.''

She saw the look of surprise. What did he think— that she liked it here? Everything she had cherished had been taken away. How would he feel if it happened to him? When others were getting established in careers, starting families, buying first homes, she was relegated to a twelve-by-twelve cell. When other people went out to dinner, she had to share her meals with twelve hundred other inmates.

When others found privacy, she had none. And had to cope with fighting the sensations of claustrophobia every moment of every day.

Glancing down at his notes, he pushed the top page aside. "I didn't find the records of the appeal."

"There wasn't one."

He looked up again. "What do you mean? There is always an appeal. It's standard procedure in a murder case."

She shrugged. "My attorney died shortly after the trial, before he could file an appeal. I applied to one or two defense attornies but they said they couldn't take me on. After a while, I just stopped trying."

She had had such high hopes every time, only to have them dashed when the lawyers she contacted refused the case. She could still remember her disbelief that no one was going to help her, that an innocent woman could be sent to prison.

"Harry Lind was your attorney."

"Yes. He was recommended to me by the ACLU when I asked for counsel. He took some cases pro bono. I was his charity that month. He died right after I came down here."

"That explains why I couldn't locate Lind when I tried."

"Why would you want to?"

"To discuss the case."

"Exactly why are you here? Aren't you still with the D.A.'s office? Do you do follow-up visits on everyone you send away, or only those you get falsely convicted?" The injustice of it all flared up. She still raged inside at the flagrant *wrongness* of the verdict.

"I'm trying to determine if we had all the facts eight years ago," he hedged.

"I thought you were sure as God about that, Mr. Walker. Michael Denning was."

He held her gaze for a long moment.

Susannah wished she knew what he was thinking. Why look into a case eight years old? One, moreover, that should have been stamped solved?

"Three days ago someone told me a friend of theirs had seen Timothy Winters in San Francisco."

Susannah stared at him, almost afraid to believe her ears. Her heart skipped a beat. The room faded from view as she stared at the man who sat so arrogantly across from her.

Timothy had been found?

Hope sparked for a brief moment. Freedom. She had the chance of freedom—

The reality of the situation slammed into her. There would be no freedom. This man was merely toying with her, as the lead prosecutor had when she had been on the stand. Michael Denning had badgered her and harangued until she hadn't known which way was up. Then mocked her claims until no one in the courtroom believed a word she said.

"And you had to rush right down here to check it out? From your great desire to get me free, I'm sure," she said scathingly. She had no trust in the legal system, or those who worked in it.

"No, from my desire to see that justice is done."

"Ha, more likely to cover up any traces of errors

so your perfect record of convictions isn't corrupted,'' she snapped back.

''If I can get you out of here, I would think you'd want to do anything you could to help me,'' he said.

''Damn you!'' She surged to her feet, anger building until she wanted to smash a chair across his handsome face. ''How dare you come here and tell me such a thing!''

Slowly Jared rose, obviously surprised by her reaction. ''I thought you'd be pleased to hear there's a chance—''

''There's no chance in hell. If you believed Timothy was seen, you would have called the San Francisco cops to get it confirmed, not come here to talk to me. I can only repeat what I said at the time. What you have written down in front of you. What do you get from giving me some sort of false hope? Do you know how cruel that is? I'm locked up *for the rest of my life* because of you. Now you come and taunt me with the unsubstantiated rumor that Timothy might be alive. What do you get from saying someone *thinks* they saw someone who *looks* like Timothy?''

''I thought you might like to know there's a chance you could be free before long.''

''And an equal chance I won't. That's what's so damn cruel!'' She gulped air, feeling light-headed. How dare he come here and taunt her.

''Wouldn't you rather think you might get free and give me some help in this?'' From his clipped tones, she knew he wasn't pleased with the way the interview was going. Tough.

She leaned against the table. "Let me tell you something, Mr. Hotshot Assistant D.A. It takes all I have to keep from going stark-raving bonkers in here every single day. I hate it. I hate it!" She banged her fists on the table, her voice rising as she screamed at him.

"But what would you know about it? You with your fancy clothes, big bucks salary and power trip that won't quit. Don't dangle false hope in front of me. I hate being here for something I never did. I hate you for sending me here. I hate being confined, being told every move to make. *I hate it!*"

The guard opened the door. "Everything all right here?"

"Fine." Jared never took his eyes from Susannah. "I can handle this, officer."

The door closed, but the guard remained beside it, watching Susannah's every move.

"I'm sorry if this is upsetting you, but I need as much information as I can get to help you." He rose and stepped around the table, blocking the guard's direct view of Susannah.

Breasts heaving, she glared at him. "You go to hell. You helped me right into this prison. You stole everything from me. My youth, my life, my family. I'm almost thirty years old and have nothing! All because you and that other man had to make names for yourselves. A conviction so your boss could get reelected, so you could keep your job and work your own way up the ladder of success, no matter who you stepped on to get there. I wouldn't trust you as far as I could throw you!''

''You need to calm down so you can talk to me,'' he said, his eyes holding hers.

She wanted to hit out, to relieve years of frustration and pain. But once she started, she might never stop.

''I don't want to talk to you. I must have some rights, somewhere.'' Tears of anger spilled down her cheek. Susannah hated that, but she stood tall and proud, glaring at him through the shimmering haze. Could she leave? Did she have to stay here and listen to him?

''Susannah.'' He reached out. She shied back instinctively.

''Don't touch me. Don't touch me.'' She scrambled away from him, pulling chairs out to impede any movement on his part. Once the table was between them again, she stopped.

Jared stood still, hands raised slightly. ''I won't touch you. Just calm down.'' Slowly he withdrew a clean handkerchief and handed it to her across the table. She stared at it for a long moment, as if suspecting a trick. He dropped it on the table and took a step back. Then she reached for it and wiped her face.

''Can I go now?'' she asked petulantly. She wanted to escape to the outside, try to regain a modicum of the peace she felt when she was on her own with the earth and plants.

"I need you to answer a few more questions." He returned to his chair, sat down and drew the notepad closer. Susannah slowly stepped around the table, keeping the maximum distance between them.

Ignoring her defiance, he asked, "You and Shawn Anderson and Timothy Winters were friends, correct?"

She nodded, wadding the handkerchief up in one hand, watching him warily.

"Actually," she cleared her throat, the strain of tears still evident. "Actually, Timothy and Shawn were friends from high school. I met Shawn when I was a senior at the university. We'd only known each other a few months when we got engaged."

Tears threatened again. She'd been so blissfully happy. She'd had a new job lined up, starting that September as a primary-schoolteacher. She'd been so in love with a wonderful man. They had just moved into their first apartment. The thought of marriage to Shawn had seemed like a dream.

Only it had shattered into a nightmare from which she still had not awakened.

"I met Timothy when we moved to Denver that June after graduation."

"Did you three spend a lot of time together?"

She shrugged. "I guess. He and Shawn were really close. Lots of nights the three of us would eat dinner and watch TV or talk or play cards. Sometimes we went out.''

"In those talks, did Timothy ever mention San Francisco, say that he wanted to go there?''

She eased a chair away from the table and sat down on the edge. Was this on the up-and-up? Was he really trying to find out the truth at this late date?

Thoughtfully she considered his question. It was hard to remember back so many years. With all they'd talked about, getting jobs, making their fortunes, setting the world on fire, any comment he might have made would have been unremarkable.

"Not San Francisco, but California once," she replied, remembering a conversation they'd had one night after a huge spaghetti dinner.

Jared's attention caught. "What about California?''

"He raved about what a good place it was, free and open. People weren't caught up in old traditions and family myths and rigid narrow opinions. It was young and vibrant and tolerant.''

"Tolerant?''

She shrugged. "I don't remember the exact words, only the feeling I picked up from his talking. Timothy was constantly being pressured by his father. I think he thought of California as a place to be himself, do his own thing, without all that pressure.''

"Did he have any friends there?''

"I don't know. He may have. I remember Shawn saying we could all descend on Sammie and have her show us Disneyland. So there must have been someone they both knew. Maybe they both had friends there. If he mentioned any names, I don't remember.''

"Except Sammie?"

She nodded. ''It's a man's name, and she's a woman. I guess that's why it stuck.''

"Timothy didn't get along with his family?'' Jared asked casually. ''That didn't come up at the trial.''

She shrugged. ''He didn't get on with his father. They hadn't seen each other in months. Timothy felt he let his father down, couldn't live up to his impossible demands and high expectations. I guess his father agreed. They had some horrendous fights, according to Shawn.''

"Do you think his father killed him?'' Jared asked, watching her closely.

She shook her head. ''I don't know, but if the gun you found was the murder weapon like you said at the trial, then no one killed Timothy. He walked away from my apartment alive and well.''

"Maybe to return home to be killed.''

"Maybe, but I didn't do it.''

"Hadn't you accused him of killing your fiancé just a week earlier when he showed up at Shawn Anderson's funeral? The local news had a field day with their videotape of your threats. Vilifying one of Denver's leading families was headline news. You threatened him with dire consequences if you ever saw his face again. Why would he come anywhere near you?''

She traced an invisible pattern on the table with a

fingertip, her eyes watching the movement, remembering.

"I said that, but I was upset. Timothy knew it. He came to see me to make sure I was all right. I told him I was sorry I had blown up. I have a tendency to do that." Or did have. Living under the strict rules of prison had knocked that out of her, except for the seething rage that sometimes built until she thought she would explode.

"When was this?" he asked.

She shrugged. "The night he was killed, as I said at the trial."

"So you two made up?" He couldn't keep the skepticism from his voice, and she heard it. Raising her gaze to him, her expression grew hard. What was the point, he didn't believe her any more today than anyone had at the trial.

"I didn't kill Timothy. He caused Shawn's death, but I have accepted it was truly an accident. Timothy was just as sorry as I was that Shawn died. They'd been friends for years."

JARED DID NOT NEED to go over the testimony again. Michael had asked enough questions eight years ago. Yet the answers didn't make the same sense. Maybe it was the experience he'd gained in the intervening years, but in reviewing the transcript, he'd found areas he couldn't believe Michael had pursued or the judge had allowed. He could punch holes in most of it today.

Staring at Susannah Chapman, he couldn't get around the fact the murder weapon had been found behind her apartment building when the police arrived the next morning. Surely if she'd killed the man the first thing she would have done was get rid of the weapon. Maybe she thought she would have plenty of time to dispose of it. Or maybe it was just a case of a criminal forgetting something that ends up fouling up a perfect crime. Sometimes the most obvious was overlooked.

He'd wasted his time. She hadn't told him anything he didn't already know. Following routine, they'd had Timothy's own father confirm that the body was his son's. Timothy had no fingerprints on record. The fingerprints of the victim had matched those found in the house. Though Michael had not used the then-new science of DNA testing, there had seemed to be no need with a positive ID. The blood type had been O positive, same as Gerald Winters's. Not once had the suspicion risen it was not Timothy who had been killed.

Susannah had a motive, opportunity and the murder weapon.

The man in San Francisco looked like Timothy. Everyone had people who looked like them. Though why he had disappeared the same day the Burroughs had called to him remained suspicious.

All in all, Jared was beginning to feel he was on a wild-goose chase. There was nothing to change the facts as they had been presented eight years ago.

"I'll be in touch if we find Timothy," he said, slipping the notebook into the folder, placing the stack into the briefcase. He was glad he hadn't mentioned anything to Steve. No sense opening a can of worms unless he'd found concrete evidence to reopen the case. Nothing today convinced him, though enough mistakes had been made in the case to warrant another look. He was appalled at how sloppy Michael's investigation had been in his haste to get a conviction. But in the end it didn't look as if it mattered.

Still, there would be time enough to open a new investigation if and when the San Francisco police came up with John Wiley and they knew for certain who the man was.

"I bet." She hadn't moved, yet once again his eyes were drawn to her. She had elegant bone structure. With an additional twenty pounds or so, she'd be beautiful. What a waste.

Were the outer trappings hiding what was inside— a cold-blooded murderer?

He stood, driven to shatter that mask. There was no other reason for him to say what he did.

"I heard you had a baby. Was it Shawn's? Or Timothy's?"

The blood left her face until her skin became so pale he thought she would faint. Never in all his years dealing with people in crisis had he seen such pain as flashed across her face. She closed her eyes and swallowed hard. Standing, she snatched up her jacket, looked through him and headed for the door.

Guilt pierced him sharp and true. But he wanted some reaction, and this line of questioning had just occurred to him. Maybe there was more between them than Timothy causing Shawn's death.

She stopped near the door and looked at him. "The baby was Shawn's, of course. I already know you think I'm a murderer, now you think I'm a whore? The baby was mine and Shawn's. Timothy didn't sleep with women."

She opened the door and the guard stepped beside her. "I think I'm going to be sick," she said.

"Wait! What do you mean Timothy didn't sleep with women?" Jared hurried to the door.

She turned. "And you're supposed to be such a hotshot attorney," she said scathingly. "He was gay."

Thunderstruck, Jared stared after her as she and the guard walked down the hall.

Gay! There had been nothing about that anywhere in the investigation, the court case, none of his notes. He had married into the family, and never heard a whisper of a rumor to that effect.

Had that been something else Michael had hushed up? Jared returned to the table and snapped his case closed. He walked into the hall, in time to see the guard open the heavy door that led to the cells. His last glimpse of Susannah Chapman was as she hurried through.

When Jared reached the interstate, he set the cruise control and tried to think through the startling revelation.

Would the fact Timothy Winters was gay have any bearing on the murder? The thought had never crossed his mind.

Yet he couldn't deny San Francisco had long been known as the mecca of homosexuality in America, it beckoned like a light to those who didn't find acceptance in their hometowns. Had Timothy been drawn there because of it?

For a moment he played with the idea that Timothy had left that night, not knowing someone had been killed in his house.

But it didn't work. He would have contacted someone in the intervening years. Would have used his own money to tide him over until he obtained a job.

Timothy's body had been identified. The gun had matched the murder weapon type, but with a shotgun, positive correlation was impossible. The blood on the barrel matched the victim. The gun behind Susannah's apartment building had been registered to Timothy Winters. A second shotgun had never been found. There was no getting around any of it as long as it was Timothy who lay dead and buried.

But what if it hadn't been Timothy who had been killed? What if Timothy had done the killing and left the gun at Susannah's before disappearing from Denver? With a murder rap hanging over his head, he'd be a fool to contact his family. Had the identification been wrong? Had Timothy not been the victim but the killer?

Pulling over into a rest area, Jared scrambled through the file, seeking information in the notes and transcripts he'd brought along. It had been a hasty, rushed investigation, ending prematurely when Michael had declared he had enough evidence to try Susannah Chapman when that unexpected slot opened.

He'd been determined to get a conviction before the elections. And he had succeeded.

Dammit! Jared stared off into the afternoon. Had the identification been wrong? Timothy's father, Gerald Winters, had died five years ago. It was impossible to question him further. There were other ways to prove the identity of the corpse at this late date, but they would have to exhume the body. And without a stronger reason than he had, he wasn't sure he'd get a court order.

Was Timothy really living in San Francisco as the Burroughs believed, and not buried in the family plot in the cemetery on the far side of town as everyone else had thought for the past eight years?

If Susannah had been telling the truth all along that she was innocent, he had been instrumental in sending a woman to prison for a crime she hadn't committed.

CHAPTER THREE

NOELLE SMILED at Martin as she handed him an after-dinner cup of coffee. Idly she let her eyes drift around the room. She loved her house—she loved the elegance, the decor, but she especially loved that this was the home she'd shared with Jared.

"And what is that smile about?" Martin asked. His salt-and-pepper hair gleamed in the lamplight. His rugged, tanned face was turned to her, as if she were the most important thing in the room.

"I was just thinking how much I like this house."

"It is charming, a perfect background for its exciting and stunning owner."

Her smile broadened. "You always have a way with words." He always had the perfect compliment, the correct turn of phrase. And she was only human. After Jared left, she'd suffered doubts about her own desirability—and Martin went a long way to assuage those doubts. She was fond of him. He was a distinguished-looking man, but he wasn't Jared. Why did she still yearn for her ex-husband? He'd made it clear when he moved out that he was no longer interested in her. Was her obsession with Jared merely a desire for the unattainable?

"Charming enough to marry?" Martin asked.

Dropping her gaze to the cup in her hand, she took a deep breath, her fingers trembling slightly.

"A proposal, Martin?" she asked.

"Marry me, Noelle."

She shouldn't keep him dangling. What if he gave up and turned to someone else? The silence dragged out. She had to say something. But what?

She couldn't bring herself to commit. If there were the slightest possibility that Jared would reconsider, that he'd want to live with her again, she had to be free to take him up on it.

"I need a little time," she murmured. "You caught me by surprise." She hoped he'd grant her that time. If pressed tonight, she'd have to say no.

"You may have as much time as you wish, my dear. I'm not going anywhere," he said.

The doorbell sounded, bringing Noelle's eyes up.

"Expecting someone?" Martin asked.

"No." She set her cup down and rose. Walking across the living room to the foyer, she wondered who would come calling at ten o'clock at night?

"Jared?" He was the last person she expected when she opened the door. Her mind raced with the reasons he'd come. They'd had dinner last week with Eric. He hadn't mentioned anything about coming to see him this week. Besides, it was late, Eric was in bed.

"I need to talk to you, Noelle," Jared said, closing the door behind him.

"Tonight? I have company."

"I know Martin is here, I saw his car. It won't take too long. It's about Timothy."

"Jared." Martin greeted him as he crossed the foyer.

"Martin." Jared shook the older man's hand. "Sorry to come by so late, but I need to talk to Noelle for a few minutes about her cousin, Timothy Winters."

"The cousin who died years ago? Wasn't he murdered?" Martin asked.

She nodded and looked at Jared. "Surely this could wait."

"Maybe, but I didn't want to wait." He turned to Martin. "Some friends of Noelle's parents believe they saw Timothy in San Francisco a couple of weeks ago. We're looking into it."

"You are?"

She had not expected this, he knew. She'd probably assumed he would try to cover everything up—at least until after the elections. She had never fully grasped his passion for justice.

He nodded. "I have a few questions for you."

"Martin, I—"

"It's all right, darling. I'll make myself at home until you two are finished. Take Jared into the study and answer his questions. I'll be around if you need me." Martin nodded to Jared and returned to the living room.

Noelle led the way. The room they entered had

been his office. She'd been thrilled when her father had patterned it after an English manor library as a wedding gift. The desk was huge, bare and gleaming in the light. When Jared had used the room, it had been piled high with papers, legal briefs and law books.

He automatically sat behind the desk. Opening his case, he pulled out his thick folder and a notebook.

"Is it really possible Don and Fran Burroughs saw Timothy?" she asked.

"If Timothy is alive, I need to find him and discover the truth about what happened that night," Jared said.

"If he is alive, the conviction that you obtained would be thrown out. That kind of publicity could prove a catastrophe with the elections less than four weeks away," she said thoughtfully.

He leaned back in the chair and regarded her. "Do you think I care about Steve Johnson's chance for reelection when I may have been responsible for sending an innocent woman to prison?"

She shrugged. "Michael Denning was relentless at the trial. He wanted a conviction at all costs."

"Not at any cost. I helped Michael win the conviction of a murderer. I wanted to prove myself to you and your family. Maybe I wanted the conviction so badly I thought of little else. It was my first major case. But I also sincerely believed we were right. Now it turns out we could have been completely wrong."

She shrugged. "And if you were—wrong, I mean?"

He sighed. "I do my job because I'm looking for justice. If justice was miscarried, it needs to be corrected. Publicity and elections are secondary, Noelle. You know how I feel about that."

"The white knight rushing off to save the fair maiden. You have always been such an idealist."

"Sit down, Noelle, answer my questions and I'll get out of here as quickly as I can."

"What questions do you have that couldn't have waited until tomorrow?"

"Your uncle identified Timothy's body, or rather he identified the body as Timothy," Jared began.

She nodded. "What was left of it. I didn't see it, of course, but Michael was disgustingly graphic at the trial."

"A shotgun blast to the face does tend to eradicate features."

"I don't need it brought up again. Uncle Gerald identified the body. The man the Burroughs saw had to be someone else."

"Do you know how he did it?"

"What?"

"How did Gerald know it was Timothy? There was no face left, most of his jaw was gone."

"Jared, please. How should I know? It wasn't something Uncle Gerald discussed with the rest of the family. He must have seen something that let him know it was Timothy."

Jared looked at his notes. ''The body was six feet tall, had dark hair, no distinguishing marks, aside from the fact the face had been blown away.'' He glanced up briefly. ''Sorry. I'm trying to find out why Gerald thought it was Timothy. I wish I had asked him at the time.''

Noelle crossed her legs and leaned back. ''We don't know it wasn't Timothy. As you said, the Burroughs could have seen a man who resembled him. It's logical that the man who was murdered was Timothy. He was wearing his clothes, was found in his house. He was as tall as Timothy, had dark hair. He was wearing the family ring. Sounds pretty convincing to me.''

Jared nodded, ticking a check by a notation on the sheet before him. ''I guess. The ring and earring were returned to your uncle. Do you know what he did with them?''

''Earring?''

He looked up at her tone. ''The pierced earring from his right ear.''

''Timothy didn't wear an earring. Are you crazy? My uncle would have had a fit if he even thought a son of his considered such a thing. Timothy would never have done something like that.''

Jared sat back staring at her. ''Are you sure Timothy didn't wear one?''

''Absolutely positive. We had dinner together the week before the murder. I would have noticed. Uncle

Gerald would have noticed, and not let it gone unchallenged.''

"Timothy could have taken it out for dinner."

She rose and leaned over the desk, reaching up to unfasten one of her own earrings. Tucking her short hair behind her ear, she tilted her head and pointed.

"You can see the hole even if the earring is removed. Believe me I would have definitely noticed if Timothy had a hole in his lobe."

She sat back down and reinserted the earring.

"I learned today that Timothy was gay," Jared said.

Noelle froze, her eyes locked with his. Slowly her hands lowered into her lap.

"Are you sure? If Uncle Gerald had found out, he would have killed Timothy himself," she murmured.

"You didn't suspect?"

She thought for a moment. "No. Yet, now that you say it, it would explain some things. Timothy dated a lot of girls, but never became serious about any of them. Never went steady as I remember, even in high school. Knowing he was gay would have killed his father." Noelle frowned. "Uncle Gerald had such strong beliefs about the duties of a Winters, the responsibilities and our position in the community."

"I take it your Uncle Gerald wasn't the most tolerant of men."

"Not for something like that. Any more than my father is. Jared, if the corpse truly wore an earring, it wasn't Timothy. How could Uncle Gerald have missed that?''

"Clothing and jewelry are removed. Gerald was given the ring, the earring—maybe he thought the earring was a random one someone had dropped and Timothy picked up. He was wearing the Winters's family ring, maybe that's all Gerald focused on.''

"So doesn't that prove it was Timothy? Maybe he had his ear pierced after that dinner party. Though how he planned to tell his father, I haven't a clue.''

"The more I discover, the more I'm starting to believe that Timothy Winters is not the man buried in that cemetery plot. I believe I have enough to request exhumation of the body and DNA testing, if the family doesn't object.''

THIS WAS NOT the topic of conversation Noelle wanted with him. Why couldn't Jared look at her with as much intensity as he studied his notes? Why couldn't he have been the one to ask her to marry him tonight instead of Martin.

"We need to investigate until we get an answer one way or another.'' Jared rose, snapping shut the briefcase.

She saw any advantage slipping away. Maybe she should give up and consider Martin's proposal.

Noelle walked him to the front door, and watched as Jared took the flagstone walkway to his car. He never looked back.

Sighing, she shut the door.

"Problems, darling?" Martin stood in the archway to the living room.

"I don't know. Jared thinks it might not have been Timothy who was killed eight years ago." She shivered. She didn't want to think about the publicity that announcement would bring. She especially didn't want to have to deal with reporters questioning her. Didn't want to have everyone speculating about who the murdered man was and why her cousin had dropped out of sight for so long.

"Why does he think that?" Martin asked, startled.

She looked at him, then walked past him into the living room. "Come and sit down, Martin, and I'll tell you what I know." He deserved to know everything she did. After all, she might end up marrying him one day.

JARED SWUNG BY his office. There were a couple of lights on in the building, none on his floor. It was late. But he couldn't rest now. If Timothy wasn't the victim, Susannah most likely wasn't a murderer. The strongest tie connecting her was the motive—grief and anger over Timothy's involvement in Shawn Anderson's death. That damning tape the local station played over and over had clinched it. A grief-stricken woman wildly threatening Timothy Winters, and two weeks later he was dead.

When he reached his office, he saw the fax on top of his desk. Rose knew what he was working on. The fax was of a set of fingerprints. The originals would be sent express mail, but this copy might provide enough for the local police to begin work. Did the records of all the prints from Timothy's apartment remain on file?

He stared at the sheets remembering what Don Burroughs had said when Jared had talked with him.

"I never thought she did it, you know," Don had confided.

"Who?" Jared had asked.

"The blonde accused of the murder. She looked too young, too baffled by everything to be a cold-blooded murderer. The verdict surprised me. Of course, that prosecutor was relentless, and so very sure of himself. I'm sure that had a lot to do with the jury's decision. And her attorney wasn't any good."

"He was ill," Jared said aloud. Too ill to prepare a good defense?

Had there been other clues he'd overlooked that might have tempered Michael's fevour for the case, prevented Michael from twisting Susannah's words until her version was ineffective and worthless and then could convince twelve men and women that she had killed a man?

It didn't matter. It was time to talk to Steve. Jared had enough evidence to reopen the case. And Jared wanted to be the one in charge. If he had screwed up eight years ago, he needed the chance now to make it right.

He'd then probably spend the rest of his life trying to atone for his mistake.

He tilted back in his chair and gazed out into the night. He was protected from any lawsuit. He'd done his job to the best of his ability. She had no recourse against him or Michael, had he lived, or the state of Colorado.

Yet it seemed grossly unfair. She'd lost eight years of her life, had no money, no job, no home. Had given her baby up for adoption. The state would apologize and cut her loose.

Where would she go? How would she manage for the first few months until she got on her feet? He couldn't even imagine the magnitude of the endeavor. But he would help in any way he could. It would never make up for the wrong, but it was all he could do.

SUSANNAH LAY on her bed, staring into the dark. Ever since Jared Walker had visited her, she had begun to hope there would be an end to the nightmare. Had someone truly seen Timothy? Would she get a new trial? Or would the district attorney just hush it up and sweep it under the carpet?

She turned on her side, afraid to hope, unable to keep from doing so. The thought of being free from prison, to go where she wanted, to eat what she wished, to get away from the confinement when the walls closed in was almost too overwhelming.

She hugged the thought to herself. She hadn't even told Marissa. The crushing disappointment would be more than she could bear if it all turned to naught.

There had to be a good possibility, or why would Jared Walker have come to see her in person?

Just before drifting to sleep, she wondered about the man himself. He believed in justice. But would he fight as hard for her as he had against her?

CHAPTER FOUR

A COUPLE OF WEEKS LATER, Jared sat at his desk and tried to concentrate on the brief he was reviewing, but his mind couldn't focus. He tried to ignore the ticking of the wall clock, ignore the minutes as they crept toward two.

He threw down the papers and rose, striding to his window. His fist hit the frame. He should be at the courthouse. He should be the one petitioning the judge. He should be the one setting the final stage to obtain Susannah Chapman's release.

Instead, he was stuck here in his office as if it were any other day, while Steve Johnson presented the facts to the judge that ought to set an innocent woman free. Of course Steve had insisted—it was a grandstand play for the elections, now only days away.

Jared turned and paced his office. He had wanted to call Susannah and let her know what was happening, but Steve had told him in no uncertain terms he was not to contact her. The past two weeks had been hectic with discovery. The DNA tests had been rushed through, proving the murdered man had not been Timothy Winters. The search continued for the man in California. Combined with the irregularities of the initial investigation, Steve felt they had enough evidence to request a judge overturn the conviction, expunge her record and set Susannah free. There would be no retrial. Steve Johnson believed, at least publicly, that Susannah Chapman was an innocent woman.

Jared was the one who had initiated the change, he should have been the one at her side. He wanted her to know that he recognized the wrong and had done what he could to right it.

Steve had not seen it that way. In his opinion, the wrongful conviction had been done during Michael Denning's term, and Jared had been Michael's right-hand man at the trial. Steve insisted it would be better to show the people of Denver that the incumbent was the one delving into the situation, righting the wrong of his predecessor.

That was the important aspect, Jared reminded himself. That the wrong was righted. That she was freed.

He knew so little about her. Only the facts from the original investigation, and the bit of information he'd learned when he visited the prison. But her face haunted him. Her eyes held a mysterious appeal he couldn't begin to explain.

What had she dreamed about before all this happened? What plans had she made and lost? She'd given up her baby thinking she would be incarcerated for life. He couldn't imagine not seeing Eric for eight years, much less the rest of his life.

How she must hate everyone connected with the

trial. How long would it take to erase the nightmare of memories she must harbor. Would she ever?

He flicked a glance at the clock. Ten after two. She was in the chambers, Steve would be presenting the evidence to the judge.

In his mind he followed the proceedings.

Steve would present the information Jared had discovered. The comparison of prints the Denver police had kept on file. There had been two sets of prints throughout Timothy's house. Neither set had ever been identified. But the ones taken from John Wiley's workstation matched one set. The other belonged to the dead man.

Next would come Noelle's recent deposition that her cousin had not had a pierced ear. That the family had not known he was gay.

The DNA test results would follow. With the proof the man was not Timothy Winters, all motive for Susannah as a killer would vanish.

The circumstantial aspect of the evidence would be reviewed. The gun had not been in her possession, only near her home. There were no prints of hers anywhere on the gun or in Timothy's house or the front door.

The judge would review the new data, listen to the recommendation of the district attorney, and in all likelihood turn to Susannah and say the words that would give her back her life.

Then she would thank Steve and walk away, free after eight years.

Where would she go?

Would he ever get a chance to expunge his own guilt and atone for his part in robbing her of those eight years?

He reached for his phone and dialed his secretary. "Is Steve back yet?"

"No, Jared. I believe you told me to let you know the minute he walked in. I am planning to do so." Rose's voice was patient.

He hung up, and sat down, staring at the stack of work needing his attention. He couldn't concentrate. He waited impatiently for Steve to return. He paced.

He glanced at the clock just as the phone rang—two-forty.

"Steve's back," Rose said succinctly.

In three minutes Jared was in Steve's office.

"How did it go?"

"Like clockwork. It didn't take ten minutes. Of course, then I had to handle the press."

"The press?"

"They claimed to know the facts. Asked what I planned to do about you. Did I suspect anything had been blatantly mishandled in the trial? Had Michael Denning or you been bought off by the Winters family? Was evidence suppressed to get a conviction? The usual B.S. in a situation like this. Have we issued a new warrant now for the murderer? Who was the real victim? We need to make this case a priority. At the least, get the victim identified. They knew a hell of a lot."

"How did Susannah react?"

"She appeared to be stunned by the onslaught. I think she was grateful to be taken back to jail."

"Back to jail?" Jared felt as if he'd been kicked in the gut. He'd been so sure the judge would release her. Certain the evidence they'd uncovered was enough to get the conviction overturned.

"You know she had to go to the city jail to be processed out. I bet the vultures of the press are camped there right now, ready to devour her. She looks like a strong wind would blow her away." Steve took his chair behind his desk, studying Jared.

"It went as planned, then," Jared said.

Steve nodded, his expression grave. "Judge Forsythe felt the new information was sufficient to overturn the previous ruling. He was a bit scathing in his comments about how this office had let the case get as far as a trial. I reminded him I wasn't the D.A. at the time."

"What will she do now?" Jared asked.

"I have no idea, probably sell her story to the tabloids for a fabulous sum of money. This close to the election, I think for the time being, you should make yourself scarce. Unless, of course, you want to be cross-examined by the media?"

Jared shook his head.

"I think my interview went well, but if you've cost me this election, Walker, I'll have your job before I leave," Steve said in dismissal.

It was no more than Jared expected. Steve was in

for the long haul in politics and a second term as district attorney was only the beginning. If he went down, he'd sure as hell take down the man who'd caused his fall.

SUSANNAH COULDN'T BELIEVE she was stalling. Once the judge pronounced her free, she thought she would sail out of the courtroom and begin her life again. Reality was as scary as the nightmare she'd been living. Now she relished the privacy she found in the restroom.

They had given her a change of clothing. She checked herself in the mirror. The shirt and jeans were loose. The shoes fit, however. And anything was better than prison garb. Biting her lips, she wished she looked better. She was too thin as Jared Walker had commented—was it only a couple of weeks ago?

He hadn't shown up at the hearing. She refused to admit she'd been disappointed. She'd wanted the judge to blast him as he had the district attorney. Have him disbarred or slapped in jail for contempt or something.

Now she was free.

And scared.

Overwhelmed by the gaggle of newspaper reporters and television cameramen at the courthouse, she had sought the protection of the correctional officers to shelter her from the barrage of questions and speculation.

Fortunately she had to be processed out. It hadn't taken long, but still she stalled.

"You all right?" One of the female correctional officers stepped into the restroom. "You've been in here a long time."

"I'm fine." Susannah tried to smile, tried to feel fine. She could walk out of the jail and do anything she wanted. Except, she didn't have a clue what to do first—besides escape the media.

The woman studied her sympathetically. "I don't blame you for not wanting to go out there. I wouldn't like to face that crowd. Tell you what. I'll take you down through the garage to the other building, let you out a back door. You can give them the slip for a while."

"Would you?" Her first thought was, what was in it for the woman. Then she stopped herself. Maybe the offer was one of genuine kindness. She had to stop looking for hidden meaning in everything if she was going to make it on the outside.

"I'd appreciate that." Taking a deep breath, Susannah stepped forward, unsure and unready to face her future, but a free woman.

JARED EASED his car from the parking space and turned toward the street. Pausing at the driveway, he debated which way to go. Right would take him home. Left would point him toward the city jail.

He wanted to see her again, once, to confirm she

was all right. That she was truly free to take up her life again.

The life he'd interrupted.

He turned left.

In seconds he drove down Cheyenne Street, appalled at the number of reporters milling in the courtyard in front of the police building. Slowly he sought a glimpse of Susannah. But she had obviously not come out yet. The reporters lurked, ready to pounce when she showed—to wring every ounce of sensationalism they could from this unexpected and unusual event.

Turning his head in case someone recognized him, he sped away. He would not add to the paparazzi's feeding frenzy by stopping. He knew it was only a matter of time before some enterprising reporter cornered him. He hoped it would be after Steve held his press conference, after the press finished with Susannah. There was nothing he could add.

Turning toward the Capitol building, he hadn't gone a block before he saw her, walking briskly along the sidewalk. Her hair was still too short, and she wore a thin denim jacket, a yellow shirt and jeans that were too big for her.

Jared glanced behind him, slowed his car and lowered the passenger-side window.

"Susannah Chapman!" he called, stopping dead in the middle of the lane.

SUSANNAH HEARD her name and looked around, warily. Hadn't she escaped the news media after all?

Then she saw him, leaning across his seat, calling her through an open car window.

She didn't have to talk to him.

Almost giddy with the knowledge that she didn't ever have to talk to him, she resumed walking. She could do anything she wanted now. She didn't have to answer to anyone.

"Susannah, wait."

She increased her pace, watching as his car pulled ahead, swerved and jerked to a stop at the curb.

She wanted nothing from him. He'd put her in prison.

Then he'd gotten her out.

She wished there was a way to take eight years of his life from him, to lock him up and see how he liked it. To take something precious from him and destroy it forever. Did he have any children she could snatch away? Did he have a wife she could destroy and leave him reeling with loss?

She took another breath and slowly continued, her eyes watchful as he climbed out of his car and stepped onto the sidewalk ahead of her.

"I have nothing to say to you," she said, stopping several feet away.

He reached out as if to grab her arm. "I just—"

Prison-honed instincts rose instantly. "Don't touch me!" Her fists were raised, adrenaline pumped.

"I won't." He held his hands up, palm toward her. Taking a step back, he met her gaze. "I won't touch you. I just wanted to talk to you for a minute."

"I don't want to talk to you." She turned. She'd have to retrace her steps, risk the paparazzi. Anything to avoid Jared Walker.

"I want to make sure you're going to be all right."

She looked over her shoulder. The sidewalk was deserted. No sign of the press. "Why shouldn't I?"

Lowering his hands, he moved closer, staying near the curb as if not to spook her.

"Did you get some money?" he asked.

She nodded. Not a lot, but enough to tide her over until she could find a job. She hoped.

"Enough for a place to stay, food to eat, new clothes?"

Reluctantly she turned to face him. What was he up to? What did he really want? She didn't trust him an inch.

"That's none of your business," she said. "Nothing in my life is any of your business ever again."

"I just want to make sure you're okay." He took a deep breath. "I'm sorry. I'm sorry for the decision eight years ago. I'm sorry for all that went wrong."

Stunned, she stared at him. It was the last thing she'd expected.

"I want to help," he said.

"Why?"

"I feel responsible."

"You *are* responsible. You and that other prosecutor. I don't want anything from you, except for you to leave me the hell alone!" she snapped, anger ringing in her tone.

"I will. As soon as I know you're okay." His voice had an edge to it.

They stared at each other in silence, a silent battle of wills.

Jared broke first. "At least let me take you to dinner to celebrate your first night out."

Susannah blinked in astonishment. She'd been wrong. The apology had been the second to the last thing she'd expected. This definitely qualified as the last thing in the world she would have expected. He wanted to take her to dinner?

She opened her mouth to give him a blazing no, when something stopped her. She closed her mouth, glanced around. A young couple walked by, ignoring them. Traffic was light on the street.

She had no one waiting for her. No place to go. She was on her own. While she relished the idea, the reality was a bit intimidating. Maybe it wouldn't hurt to ease back into the mainstream by delaying the moment when she would be totally alone.

She didn't want to have dinner with Jared Walker. Yet ironically, he was about the only person in Denver she knew. The few friends she'd had before had most likely scattered. None had stood by her. She didn't even know if she would stay in Denver now that she was free.

But that decision could wait until tomorrow or even next week. The invitation for dinner needed a decision now.

"I'm not dressed for eating out," she said, stalling.

Why didn't she just tell him no and get him out of her life once and for all? Did she want to spend even an hour in this man's company? He was the enemy—he had prosecuted her, convicted her and robbed her of everything she held dear.

She saw him relax a little. Until that moment she hadn't realized how tense he'd been.

"It's a bit early to eat right now anyway. I thought you might want to go somewhere and shop for new clothes or something. I can drop you at the Sixteenth Street Mall."

She could get there on her own, she didn't need to—

Just then a mobile van from the local television station passed, headed for the jail. Susannah spun around, turning her back to Jared, to the street.

She had to get away from here, she was still too close, and the last thing she wanted was to have those reporters swarm around her with their questions and cameras.

"Susannah?"

"If we go right now, I'll take the ride," she said quickly.

He looked around. "What happened?"

"Channel 4 news van just passed. I don't want to be caught by all those reporters. There were so many at the courthouse. I don't want to have to talk to any of them."

Gingerly Susannah sat in the passenger seat of the luxury sedan. She held herself tightly, refusing to relax as she warily watched Jared pull out into the traffic. They were within a few blocks of the mall and arrived in only moments.

"Thank you." She thrust open the door and hopped out before he could say a word. Slamming it shut she took a deep breath when he climbed out of his side and looked at her across the roof of the car. She hadn't expected to feel so closed in on a short car ride. She felt better standing on the sidewalk.

"Dinner?" he asked again.

She was tempted, sorely tempted. Slowly she shook her head.

"With the evidence that we had at the time, we had nothing else to believe but that you were guilty. But the moment I found a reason to suspect things weren't the way I thought they were back then, I pushed this investigation. I'm trying to atone for the wrong. Somehow, let me make it up to you."

Sincerity rang raw in his voice.

"You can't make it up. You can't give me back my twenties. You can't give me back my baby. You can't give me back my belief in truth and honesty and justice. You can't erase the horrors of years spent in prison. You can't make it better!"

"I can try," he said, his voice low and strong.

"Why?" she whispered, her heart pounding again. Why did he keep pushing her? Didn't he know she wanted to be left alone?

"Because I want to believe in truth, honesty and justice. I need to find a way to make things right. To make amends, or I'll never be able to prosecute a case again. What if the next person is innocent? Or the next? My own faith in justice has been shaken. I need to balance the scales.''

''What about what *I* need? Maybe *I* need to be free of any reminder of the hell my life's been for the last eight years. Maybe *I* don't want to assuage your sense of guilt. Maybe you should wallow in it forever. Nothing you can do will make up to me what I've lost.''

''There were twelve other men and women who thought the way we thought.''

''Michael Denning convinced them to think the way you did.''

''Dinner isn't so much to ask,'' he said. ''We'll be in a public place.''

''Dinner won't make up for—''

''Dinner, yes or no?''

''All right. All right! I'll meet you here at six.'' With that she turned and stormed away, toward the stores that lined the open-air mall. Her emotions were in turmoil, maybe she could gain some sense between now and dinner.

Ninety minutes later, Susannah took another sip of her mocha and licked the whipped cream from her lip. Studying the drink, she shook her head. She'd come in to get a quick cup of coffee. She'd been shopping for over an hour and had only a few purchases to show for it. It was almost six and she wanted a cup of coffee. Only this place didn't sell coffee, they sold cappuccino, latte, mocha and a couple of combinations she couldn't begin to guess how to pronounce.

She didn't even know what each was until the young man behind the counter explained. Taking the chocolate-flavored one, she sat at a table near the large glass window and watched people stroll by.

It felt odd. She pinched her thumb, but didn't awaken. So it wasn't a dream. She was actually out on her own.

Ruefully she glanced at her packages. The purchases had been few. Prices had risen over the years, and she needed to hoard her money. She still had to get a room somewhere. The clothes she'd bought would be suitable for job interviews, she hoped. Tomorrow she would find an employment agency and begin her search.

She glanced down at the trim slacks she'd worn from the store. They fit perfectly. The tailored silk shirt looked suitable, she hoped, for dinner. The light jacket would hold her until she found a job and could afford something warmer for Denver's cold winter months. If she stayed. She shrugged, enjoying the feel of the fine material.

It was a good thing she was having dinner on Jared tonight, she thought whimsically. It saved her spending money on food.

Dinner with Jared Walker. She took another sip of the sweet beverage. She still couldn't believe she'd agreed. What would they talk about?

Atonement?

Revenge?

Finishing her mocha, Susannah gathered her packages and walked toward the parking lot. She spotted Jared's car, just where it had been earlier. Had he been waiting for her all this time? He climbed out as she drew near and opened the trunk.

"You can put your packages here so we don't have to carry them with us," he offered.

She leaned over and placed the bags in the trunk, straightening and stepping away. His mere presence overwhelmed her. He was so tall. And he radiated a certain energy that set her nerves on edge.

"There's a nice restaurant just a couple of blocks over. I thought we could eat there," he said, closing the trunk.

"Fine."

"It doesn't look like you have a lot of packages. Did you get everything you want?" he asked.

"Yes."

"I like what you're wearing now. It fits better than the jeans you wore earlier."

She nodded. Feeling as tongue-tied as a high school girl on a first date, she kept pace as he walked, but had nothing to say.

When they reached the small restaurant, he held the door for her, touching her back lightly to guide her inside. She shrank from the contact.

"I won't hurt you, Susannah," he said softly in her ear, making sure he didn't touch her.

She glanced at him, knowing the wariness showed, unable to release it.

"I don't like being touched," she said breathlessly. His face was only inches from hers. She noticed the fine lines radiating from his eyes, the hint of a five o'clock shadow, the full lower lip. His breath was sweet as it brushed across her cheek.

"I'll try to remember that."

"CHAMPAGNE," Jared said to the waiter a few minutes later after they'd been seated.

Susannah looked at him with surprise.

Jared shrugged. "I know I'm not your first choice to celebrate with, but it is your first night out and I think it calls for champagne."

She nodded, her eyes darting away to take in the quiet, elegant restaurant. The paneled walls gave an old-world ambiance, as did the fine linen tablecloths and the heavy silver place settings. Everything was first class.

She watched some of the people as they came in, as they ordered, as their food arrived. Yesterday she ate at the mess hall at the women's corrections facility. Today she was dining in a fancy restaurant in Denver.

She looked back at Jared. His gaze hadn't shifted from her.

"Thank you," she said reluctantly. She hated feeling beholden to him for anything. However, despite his part in her past, she was touched he thought her first night out was something to celebrate. She looked down at the pristine tablecloth. She didn't want to like him. She didn't want to feel anything for him but hostility and bitterness. She would never forget what he and the other prosecutors had cost her.

"If you could have spent tonight with anyone, who would it be?" he asked.

She didn't hesitate. "Marissa Hernandez. She was my cell mate. She's getting out in a couple of months. It's funny. I hated the thought of her leaving. She's my best friend. Maybe my only friend. Now I ended up getting out before she did."

She moved her fork a smidgen to the left.

"Maybe I'll have enough money to bring her here on her first night out, and we'll have champagne," Susannah said softly. Wouldn't Marissa love that!

When the champagne arrived, Jared raised his glass in a toast.

"To a bright and shining future. I wish you all the best, Susannah."

She sipped the sparkling wine and nodded. She wished herself all the best. It was time things looked up.

It was going all right, she thought a little while later. They had ordered, and Jared had been masterful at small talk. He spoke of why he liked this restaurant. Of the different kinds of restaurants around the downtown area. He mentioned several places she should try. Susannah didn't need to say anything. She sat and listened and sipped her champagne.

When dinner arrived she smiled again in pure delight. The food was artfully arranged on the plate, nothing like prison fare.

"What are your plans now?" Jared asked as she began to eat.

The niggling fear that had plagued her all day strengthened. "I'll start looking for a job first thing tomorrow. Do you think I should have started today?"

He shook his head. "You might want a few days to get used to being on your own again," he suggested.

"Can't afford it. I need to get a job right away. I'm a little low on resources."

"Do you have a place to stay?"

She hesitated as if she didn't want to reply. "Not yet. I can find a motel room tonight. I won't be able to afford an apartment until I have a job."

"I have room at my place."

The minute Jared spoke the words, Susannah felt like bolting. Had that been his reason to take her to dinner? He wanted something more, some show of gratitude for getting her out?

"Sorry, dumb idea. Forget I said it," he said quickly.

She faced him squarely, eyes flashing with anger. "Dinner is one thing. And probably a mistake. But I don't want anything else from you. Nor do I owe you anything. Do I make myself clear?"

"I'll drop you off at a nice motel when we finish and you won't have to see me again."

"Fine." She took another sip of champagne. She saw a woman at the next table smile at her. She probably thought she and Jared were celebrating something quite different.

For a moment Susannah wished things had been different. Wished some handsome man had asked her out to celebrate some wonderful occasion—a promotion, or other good news. Wished they could laugh together, maybe go dancing. Wished he would look at her with love in his eyes and that she could feel that sizzling sensation once more.

She still missed Shawn.

She could understand why the woman kept looking their way. Jared was good-looking, distinguished, and carried himself with assurance. He was probably used to women coming on to him. She glanced at his left hand. No ring. Did that mean he was single? Or just didn't wear a wedding band?

"If you contact the newspapers or some magazines, you could make some money telling your story," Jared said.

She blinked at that. "I can't believe you're suggesting I sell my story for money. You don't come off too good in it."

"I can't change what happened, Susannah. By tonight's news report, everyone in Denver will know the story. Some of Steve's interview at the courthouse was on the radio. I heard it while I waited for you.

Michael Denning and I don't show up too good however you look at it.''

"Is that the reason for dinner? Trying to bribe your way into my good graces?''

He smiled ruefully and shook his head. "I doubt that's possible. I truly didn't want you to spend tonight alone.''

She felt an odd flutter near her heart. His eyes were dark and warm as they gazed at her, honesty shining in their depths. His cheeks creased when he smiled and framed his lips. She studied the dark eyebrows that neatly arched over his eyes, the strong, stubborn jaw that feared nothing—even being proved wrong before millions of people.

"And your wife didn't mind you taking me out?'' she asked.

"I'm not married.''

"Oh.''

She ate a bit more, then said, "I don't want to talk to the reporters.''

"How about a book publisher? Maybe you could sell your story to a ghostwriter or something.''

She shrugged. "It's not very interesting to anyone but me.''

"And me.''

Heat seeped through her at the warmth in his gaze. She became aware of Jared as an exciting man, one who could probably charm innocent women into falling in with whatever plans he made.

Horrified her thoughts would ever touch on such an idea, she turned her mind to something else.

"I guess the jury members will hear that I was innocent, too," she murmured.

"Yes. I expect they will all feel as badly as I do about convicting an innocent woman."

"If they all offer to buy me dinner, I wouldn't have to cook for two weeks," she said cynically.

"And if you sell your story somewhere, you wouldn't have to worry about money for longer than two weeks."

"Are you trying to talk me into it?" she asked, putting down her fork. Wonderful as the food was, she was getting full.

"No. Just pointing out another way to make money. I suspect it's worrying you."

"I just hope I can get a job. Ex-cons have a hard time, I hear."

"You aren't, technically. Didn't Steve explain that today? Your conviction was nullified. The record expunged. You are not a convicted felon."

"Sure, just someone who spent eight years in the slammer for fun and games." The strain was evident in her voice.

"Everybody who sees the news tonight will understand you were innocent. You won't have a problem with a job."

"And if I do?" She desperately wanted to believe him, but she didn't believe in much of anything anymore. And why she would ever put her trust in this man was beyond reason. But she wanted him to say something she could believe in.

"Then you have them call me and I'll set them straight."

"Where's Timothy?" she asked. She'd been wondering ever since Jared had told her he'd been spotted in San Francisco.

"We don't know. The police are still looking for him."

"He killed that other man, didn't he?"

"There's evidence that could point in that direction," Jared said cautiously.

"Oh, that's great. Frame an innocent woman, and it's business as usual. But have the son of an old Denver family implicated and you pussyfoot around it like crazy."

"I'm not going to discuss that with you. It's not the purpose of our dinner."

Susannah glared at him, toying with her food. The filet had melted in her mouth. She was not a fool. It would be a long time before she'd be able to afford such a meal on her own. She savored every bite. But even so, she couldn't finish.

Jared insisted on ordering the largest, most chocolate-rich concoction on the menu for dessert.

Susannah simply stared as the waiter placed the double chocolate brownie with hot-fudge sauce and chocolate ice cream before her.

"I'll get sick if I eat all this." How many years

had it been since she had indulged in such a sinfully decadent dessert?

"I doubt it. Don't women love chocolate?"

"I'll gain a hundred pounds," she said as she picked up her fork and took her first bite.

"You need to put on some weight, you're too thin."

She ignored his comment. She knew she should put on weight, but it sounded too personal, too intimate to hear it from him.

She looked up, trying to assess the expression on his face. Could he possibly be telling her the truth—that he truly wanted to atone for the past? How did someone go about doing that?

Slowly, delighting in every bite, she ate her dessert.

JARED DIDN'T WANT to leave Susannah at the motel but had no choice. He pulled beneath the canopy by the office door. "This place is close to bus lines and is an easy ride to the downtown area. Will you be all right?"

"I can take care of myself. Thank you for dinner." She opened the door and gathered the packages he'd retrieved from the trunk when they left the restaurant.

"Susannah."

She glanced at him. "What?"

"If you need anything, call me, okay?" He held out his card. He'd written his home phone number and cell number on the back.

"I won't need anything. I can manage fine."

"Just in case." Since spending the evening with her, his protective instincts had risen. She might be street-smart in many regards—how could she help it given where she'd spent the past eight years. But in other areas, she was as green as a country girl on her first visit to the big city.

She was determined to be independent. He wanted to make her transition easier. Wanted to do something to erase the bitterness from her eyes. He had a feeling her eyes would haunt him for the rest of his life.

But, helpless, he had to wait for her to ask.

"I don't need anything more from you." She shut the car door and walked into the brightly lit lobby.

"Damn!" He hit the steering wheel in mounting frustration. "We're not done, not by a long shot, Susannah Chapman," he said softly as he watched her walk away.

CHAPTER FIVE

JARED WALKER came wide-awake instantly, the terror of the nightmare holding him in its grip. He fought for breath, gradually becoming aware of where he was as his eyes found familiar objects in the wash of moonlight. Consciously relaxing his muscles, he released the tension. Slowly his breathing returned to normal.

It had been years since he'd had a nightmare. The potency of this one clung to him longer than it should have.

Flinging off the covers, he rose and crossed quickly to the window. The cool autumn air chilled the lingering traces of sweat that clung to his skin.

Staring out at the muted landscape, his mind churned with the traces of the horror. Everything outside appeared gray, the light of the moon not sufficient to add color. Yet the scene soothed after the vividness of the dream. He'd been prosecuting Susannah, taunting her with a baby, showing her image after image of men with their faces blown away.

He headed for the kitchen. He wouldn't sleep anymore tonight. It was close enough to dawn that he might as well get dressed and head for work. There were always more briefs and depositions to read than he had time for in a day.

As the coffee dripped in the machine, he leaned against the kitchen counter and crossed his arms over his chest.

Dinner last night had been different from what he'd expected. Susannah had been shy, quiet. He remembered her obvious enjoyment of the meal, the quick curious glances around at the other diners, her delight in the chocolate dessert.

Getting her a room at the motel had been easy enough. Would she allow him to do more?

Flipping on the lights, he sank onto the comfortable sofa and stretched his legs out. That trial had been a long time ago. He'd been so young, so eager, so enthusiastic.

Now eight years later, jaded and tired, he questioned whether anything he'd once wanted was worth having. Day after day he prosecuted criminals. Some got put away, others walked. But he wasn't changing anything, only swimming more frantically upstream against a stronger and stronger flow of crime.

Jared leaned his head back against the cushions, resting his coffee cup on his flat belly. Steve Johnson wanted to win this election. So the pressure built again to get quick convictions, to prove to the good people of Denver that their D.A. was tough on crime.

But a flurry of convictions wasn't going to mean squat in the greater scheme of things. It wouldn't reduce the number of incidences, wouldn't stop the trend toward more sophisticated crimes. It would only look good on Steve Johnson's record as district attorney when the voters went to the polls.

Jared opened his eyes and surveyed the room. It was tastefully decorated, courtesy of an interior designer. But it had never felt like home—not like the cabin did. He'd come a long way from Denver's south side. For what?

He now had entry anywhere, mingled with the movers and shakers of Denver, could converse with anyone. He had Noelle to thank for that.

He sighed when he thought of his failed marriage. He'd thought he had had it all when he'd married Noelle. They'd done everything young successful couples should do—skied in Aspen, vacationed in Europe, mingled with others in their social circle—make that Noelle's social circle. She wouldn't be caught dead on the south side. As he got older, Jared had become bored and wanted more. Noelle didn't.

Looking back, the only good to come of the marriage was Eric.

Jared loved his little boy. Eric was probably the only person on the face of the earth Jared loved without reservation.

He hoped Eric would always return that love. That he wouldn't grow to resent his father as Jared resented his own. While he might make mistakes, Jared was careful not to make the same mistakes his old man had made. When Eric grew up, he'd know his father was there for him, helping him get what he wanted in life. Not crawling into some bottle and mocking every ambition he had.

Jared wasn't going down that path and refused to dwell on memories. He'd sought to prove to his father that he had what it took to be someone. He'd pushed and fought to excel in college, law school. Marrying Noelle had been the crowning achievement.

When Jared had finally realized what was happening, he had taken a long look at his life and made some decisions. He no longer had anything to prove to his old man. Now he wanted to be a good role model for his son. Life was more than show, and he wanted Eric to learn that lesson young.

Maybe it was time to make some more decisions.

Sipping the last of the coffee, he put the cup on the table and rose. Time to get dressed and head for work.

NOELLE WALKER stood before her mirror wearing a pink push-up bra and matching high-cut bikini panties. She studied her figure dispassionately. Except for the faint stretch marks near the bikini line, her figure was still as firm and slim as when she had been twenty-five. Or even twenty. Turning sideways, she ran her hands over the lightly tanned skin in deep satisfaction.

She had just turned thirty-two, but she didn't look a day more than twenty-eight. Frowning, she wondered how long it would last. Women didn't age as well as men.

Jared looked great at thirty-four. His frame had

filled in, was lightly muscled without looking like a weight lifter. His hair grew thick and dark, no strands of gray yet; she had her hairdresser color her gray every month. And his dark eyes always made her think of sex.

He'd probably look good until well into his sixties or seventies, while she would soon dissolve into wrinkled skin, brittle hair and a frantic exercise program to maintain her figure in a desperate attempt to hold onto her youth.

She sighed and studied her face. Martin liked it. He loved her, he claimed. Which was probably just as well since he'd proposed. He'd certainly proved generous with his time and his money.

Unlike Jared.

She should stop comparing the two. She liked Martin, sometimes even felt a burst of genuine affection. But she still *wanted* Jared. And she'd marry him again in a New York minute if he'd ask.

That was the reason she kept stalling Martin, in the faint hope that Jared would want her back.

Martin was going to be in London for several weeks. Maybe she could make one more effort to recapture Jared's affections.

JARED KISSED Eric good-night Sunday evening after he brought him home. The little boy bounded up the stairs. Smiling, Jared tried to ease the tug in his heart. He got to see his son every other weekend, and sometime during the week. It had to be enough. For all her faults, Noelle was a good mother.

"Want a brandy, darling?" Noelle asked, moving to the small bar at the side of the room.

"No, I need to get going."

"Stay for a while longer. I don't need to tuck him in for a few minutes. Stay. I was lonely this weekend."

He turned at her tone and studied her. She looked lovely tonight in a long dark green silky skirt and soft, long-sleeved shirt. Her face was framed by her deep auburn hair, and her eyes and skin glowed. Or was that makeup artistry at work?

For a moment he saw another face, gaunt and haunted. He hadn't heard from Susannah in the days since she'd been released. He'd hoped she would call for some help, but his phone remained silent every night. No messages awaited him on the answering machine when he returned home each day.

He shook his head. He was obsessing about a stranger.

"I'll stay a while, but no brandy. I have some more work to do when I get home tonight."

"You always did work too hard," she murmured, pouring herself a small snifter and gliding to the sofa. Sitting, she patted the cushion beside her. "All work makes a man dull. You never used to be dull, darling. Remember when we were first married?"

Jared met her gaze. "Of course I remember."

"We went to so many parties, had such a fun time."

He had done all the party scenes, both for the sheer triumph of finally being invited, as well as trying his best to do what he could to please his young wife.

"We're older now, Noelle. Surely you don't like to party as much as you did then." That was one of the things that had convinced him to end their marriage. They no longer shared the same ideas of what constituted fun.

She frowned and set her glass on the coffee table. "I still like to have a good time. Things changed for us when Eric was born."

He looked at her sharply. "Do you blame Eric?" He had never thought of that.

"No, of course not. But things were never the same after he was born."

"We didn't party as much, but that was because I needed to make sure I developed my career, to provide for my expanded family. I wanted to make a name for myself in the prosecutor's office. There came a point where my time was better spent in other areas than frivolous parties."

"But I had money. We didn't need to live on your salary."

"And we didn't entirely. But I wanted to be a major contributor." At her bewildered look, he smiled ruefully. "We never did understand one another in that area, did we? It doesn't matter now, Noelle."

"You make it sound like we're a hundred years old."

"Some days I feel like it," he said, leaning back on the sofa.

"Because of this thing with Timothy?" she guessed accurately.

He nodded.

"Do you think he's alive?"

"He's alive."

"You know that for sure?"

"Yes. We wired his photo to SFPD and they did a check in the office buildings along California Street where the Burroughs saw him. They found a dozen people who swear they know him as John Wiley. He disappeared the day the Burroughs spotted him and hasn't been seen since."

"Is that enough evidence?"

"The man has been in the Bay Area for about seven years, nothing prior to that is known about him. And, he's gay."

"Still—"

"His prints match the unknown ones taken from Timothy's apartment. With what we had, the judge had enough to release Susannah Chapman."

"I know. All of Denver knows. It was splashed all over the news last Thursday and Friday. It should insure Steve gets reelected."

"So he hopes," Jared said.

His cell phone rang. Jared glanced at the caller ID,

not recognizing the number. He excused himself and crossed the room to stand near the windows.

"Walker."

"I'm sorry to bother you," Susannah's voice came across softly.

"I told you to call me if you needed anything. What's up?"

"I'm at the police station near the northeast section of town. I don't have any ID and they are accusing me of soliciting. I haven't sunk *that* far. Could you vouch for me?"

"I'll be right there." He confirmed the address and clicked off the phone.

"I have to go."

"Whatever for?" Noelle asked.

"Susannah Chapman's been detained and I need to get her out of the situation."

"I saw all the media coverage," Noelle said, rising. "I thought she'd be anxious to be the center of attention, but the only shots they had of her were from a distance. I don't see any of it as newsworthy. Just distasteful. Why is she calling you? And how did she have your phone number?"

"Look around you, Noelle. You have a beautiful home and a wonderful son. You have plenty of money, more time than you need to do everything that interests you. What would you do if tomorrow it was all taken from you? How would you feel being locked away in a cell with nothing around you of your own life? And to know you would live all your years that way?''

She shivered, her gaze darting around the room.

''Because of the way Michael and I handled that trial eight years ago, we brought that very situation to an innocent woman. I gave her my phone number, and told her to call me if I could do anything to help.''

''So now you're on a quest to correct things?''

Noelle's tone rankled.

''If it were only that simple. How do you make up for taking eight years of a person's life?''

''You don't have to do it, Jared. You were just doing your job at the time. These things happen.''

He headed for the door. He hadn't communicated well with Noelle when they'd been married, why had he thought he could reach her tonight?

''I wanted you to stay,'' she said hurrying after him.

''I know you did, but it's not in the cards, Noelle. What we had burned out a long time ago.'' He paused by the front door.

''Not for me,'' she said.

''You're just annoyed I was the one who walked away before you could. Go after Martin, he loves you and wants you like crazy. Don't play around or you'll lose him, too.''

''Dammit, Jared, I don't want Martin if I can have you.''

''But you can't, that's what you don't seem to understand. I wanted you years ago. I was flattered by your attention. And you opened doors for me. I appreciate everything you did for me.''

''You loved me,'' she argued.

Nodding, he reached out to rub his thumb across her jaw, looking deep into her eyes. ''I loved you when we married. I loved you when we had Eric. It just didn't last. I can't change that. But, honestly, Noelle, do you really love me? Or am I just something you think you want because you can't have me?''

''I know what you want. You don't want to stay tonight, you want to hurry to your little jailbird,'' she bit out. ''Aren't you worried that error in your conviction record will cost you your job?''

''If it does, I'll deal with it.''

NOELLE REMAINED standing by the door long after Jared had left, her anger growing. She had practically thrown herself at him and he had walked away. Too concerned with some bitch who had gotten herself convicted of murder.

She was tired of waiting. If he didn't want her, she would finally cut her losses and take Martin. See how Jared liked that!

But if he thought he could walk away just like that, he'd find out soon enough he should have handled this evening differently.

CHAPTER SIX

IT TOOK JARED a half hour to reach the police station. He walked into the brightly lit holding area and saw Susannah instantly. She was sitting against the wall, within touching distance of the uniformed policeman watching her. Her eyes were closed. He could see her weariness and fatigue.

He hoped the media didn't hear about this. He'd been dodging phone calls and reporters' attempts to interview him all weekend. Things were beginning to die down. If they caught wind of this, all hell would break loose again.

Approaching the desk sergeant, he flashed his identification. "I'm here about Susannah Chapman."

The officer looked at the identification and then studied Jared. "She says she wasn't soliciting, just trying to find her way home. But it's a bad section of town. What would a nice woman be doing there?"

"I don't know, but if you don't have anything more than that, you can't hold her."

"She has no ID."

"She's just out of prison. Haven't you watched the news the last couple of days? Susannah Chapman was the one released last week. She probably hasn't had a chance to get a driver's license or other identification."

The man shrugged.

"Has she been charged?" Jared asked.

"No."

"Then as an attorney, I'm asking for a charge or a release."

The desk sergeant signed off on a form, asking Jared to sign as well. "She's yours. But if we catch her again, she will be charged."

In only moments Jared and Susannah stood on the sidewalk in front of the police station.

"Thank you," she said. "I can't believe a person isn't free to walk around town after dark without getting hassled by the cops. Or is it just me?"

She started to walk away.

"Wait a minute, I'll give you a ride home."

She eyed his car for a long moment, then took a deep breath. "Okay. Next time I'll stay closer to the motel."

"So why were you in that section of town tonight?" Jared asked a couple of minutes later as they drove toward Susannah's motel.

"I went for a walk and just ended up there."

"A walk? That part of town has to be six miles or more from where you're staying."

"Do you know how much freedom means to me? To enjoy the ability to just get out and walk as far as I want, with no one saying no, you can't do that, Chapman? I walked farther on Saturday. I was out until almost three in the morning. It was wonderful. Liberating.''

"Try to stay in a nicer section of town," he suggested.

"Sure, if I go to the ritzy section, they'll be afraid I'm a burglar and call the cops for that. A person can't catch a break in this town."

Jared wanted to defend Denver, but knew from her perspective, he'd just be blowing smoke.

"Did you find a job?" he asked.

She shook her head. "No matter what you thought, people don't want me. I have no experience except for the prison farm, don't have any references. The schools sure don't want me teaching their precious children."

He turned into the motel parking lot and cut the engine.

"What do you want to do?" he asked.

"Like I have a choice. I'll be lucky to get a job flipping burgers."

"What do you really want?" he repeated.

She looked at him warily, as if expecting a trick question. He wanted to reach out and hold her hand, tell her she was going to be fine. That she could lean on him until she got on her feet. But she'd already made it clear she didn't like being touched. And he was probably the last man on earth she wanted to lean on.

"What do I want? That's different from what I want to do. I went to college to be a teacher, but I don't think I could stand being cooped up inside all day. That's the problem with most jobs. But what I really *want* is my baby back. I want those eight years back. Can you fix that, Mr. Hotshot?"

"I'm sorry."

"Yeah, well sorry doesn't do much."

Jared took a deep breath. One step at a time, he told himself. "So start with the job first. Not an inside one. Want to work on a ranch? A farm? Construction?"

She shook her head, a glimmer of a smile touching her mouth. "No experience with horses, nor with a hammer. How many farms are around Denver?"

"More than you might think. How about a garden shop or something?"

He could see that caught her attention. Then defeat washed over her.

"They'd never hire me."

"I'll ask around," he suggested. He hadn't a clue what garden nurseries required of their workers, but if he could find a job for her it would help balance the scales, wouldn't it?

What he'd really like to do is bring a full smile to those lips. Would finding her baby do that?

The thought shocked him and he looked away. He didn't need her smiling at him, and he sure as hell couldn't give her back her baby. The child would be seven by now.

"Was it a boy or a girl?" he asked.

She knew instantly what he meant. "A baby girl.

I got to hold her for almost two hours. She was so precious. It was an easy delivery and everything. I wish Shawn could have seen her. I wish…'' She stopped talking.

He saw the sheen of tears. He wished things had been different, too. Guilt and remorse cut deep.

"Tell me what you like about gardening. We'll draft up a résumé and see what we can find, though with winter coming, I'm not sure many garden shops will be hiring."

She looked at him again, with that wary expression that he was getting used to.

"I can manage," she said stubbornly.

"Everyone needs some help sometime," he said easily. He knew better than to push her, but he could help—he owed her that much.

She thought about it so long he was sure she was going to refuse, hop out of the car and head inside the motel. But she surprised him.

"Okay, I'll write down everything I can think of and if you can help with a résumé, I'd appreciate it."

"How about you think on it overnight. I'll pick you up for breakfast at nine. We'll do it then."

She nodded. Bidding him a quiet good-night, she headed into the motel.

Jared sat in the car and watched her until she was out of sight. It was a small step, but he was pleased she was letting him help.

SUSANNAH WAITED inside the motel office the next morning for Jared to arrive. She had used the notepaper in her room to write all she could think of about her experience with gardens. It was all for vegetables. The prison tried to raise as much of its own produce during the summer months as possible. She knew little about flowers. Would it be enough? Were there truck farms around where she might get work?

Rain drizzled. Snow would be coming soon. Who would hire an outdoor worker at this time of year? Most places were probably cutting back. Yet she couldn't envision herself stuck in some office, or classroom, for hours on end.

When Jared slid his car to a stop in front of the office, she pushed open the glass door and dashed out.

"Good morning," he said as she climbed in.

"If you like rain."

"I do. It makes the air incredibly clear. The Front Range looks close enough to touch," Jared said, pulling the car back into traffic.

This was strictly a business meeting, she reminded herself. Despite her admonition, she was curious about the man. She knew what he did for a living, but there was more to Jared Walker than being an assistant district attorney. How much more did she really want to know?

"Have you always lived in Denver?" she asked.

"Yes. Raised on the south side."

Was there some significance in that statement?

"You?" he asked.

"No, I came here after college to be with Shawn.

He was originally from Boulder, though he completed his last two years of high school in Denver. He was a late and unexpected baby. When he started college, his parents retired to Florida. But he loved Colorado. There was never any question he wanted to settle here. His folks died before we graduated. So he could settle anywhere, and he chose Denver. More job opportunities, and he had his great friend Timothy.'' She couldn't help ending on a sardonic note. Timothy Winters had ended up being the worst thing that had ever happened to either of them.

"I want to see him when you catch him," she said.

"Why?"

"To find out why he did what he did." She couldn't fathom deliberately setting up someone to be convicted of a crime they didn't commit. Of course, after killing someone, she suspected setting someone else up was small potatoes. He'd done it for survival, undoubtedly.

"I'll see what I can do," Jared said.

She looked at him. Would he really? Or was he humoring her?

He focused on his driving so she had a chance to study the man. He was good-looking. How had he managed to avoid getting married? Surely the women in Denver weren't blind.

"Why aren't you married?" she asked.

"Been there, done that," he replied easily.

"Oh." She should have thought of that alternative. "Divorced a year and a half. And not planning to repeat the mistake.'' He glanced at her. ''I have a son, he's five.''

The pang shouldn't have hit so hard. She looked away. He had a son, she had a daughter. The difference was, he knew where his son was, what he was doing, loved and was loved by him.

She hadn't a clue where her daughter was or what she'd been told about her mother. Surely they wouldn't have told her Susannah was a killer. That would be too cruel for a child to know. Especially since it wasn't true.

The ache that was never far from her heart flared.

''I wish I could see her once more. Know she was all right,'' she said softly.

''You could try the courts. Since the entire adoption was based on a life sentence, with it overturned, things might change.''

She shook her head. ''Not unless something terrible happened. If she was adopted by loving parents, I wouldn't interfere. They are her parents now, the only ones she's ever known. I was just the birth mother. But if she's not in a happy home, then maybe.'' She longed to hold her baby. To share her memories of Shawn, and make plans for a bright future.

But she knew it would never happen.

At the very least, she wished she could make sure her little girl was happy.

''Does this suit you?'' Jared asked, parking near a coffee shop. From the looks of the crowd, it was a popular spot.

Susannah nodded, bringing her attention back to the reason for this meeting—to help her find a job. She wished she could manage on her own, but last Friday had been totally frustrating and disappointing. If that was what she was up against, she'd take help from the devil himself today. Glancing at Jared, she wondered if she were.

As the hostess showed them to a table, Susannah was surprised to find Jared greeted by several people as they wound their way through the crowded restaurant. If she'd thought about it, she would not have expected him to take her any place where people knew him.

He stopped to introduce her to one man sitting alone at a table near theirs. When they were seated, she looked at Jared.

"I'm surprised you introduced me," she said.

He raised an eyebrow. "Why not? He's a friend of mine, and now he knows you."

"I'm still surprised," she murmured, looking at the menu. For the first time since she was released from prison, Susannah felt like a normal person. Jared had introduced her to a friend, just as he would have anyone. She was eating breakfast with a man. Even if her being here with Jared was only a business meeting, it still felt good.

Once their order had been taken, she pulled out her notepaper.

"Let's eat first, shall we?" he said.

"Okay." She paused, then asked, "What's your little boy's name?"

"Eric."

"Has he started school yet?"

"He was in preschool last year, started kindergarten this fall. He loves it."

Her daughter would be in second grade, she thought. Did she like school? Was she as good a student as Susannah had been? Did she like math as Shawn had done, or was she more artistic?

"I'm glad he enjoys it. I wanted to teach primary grades. I didn't care if it was kindergarten or third grade." How long ago that had been. When life had been so full of promise. Now she just wanted to make it through the end of the week.

"You still can," he said.

"You make it sound easy, do what you want. But things have changed. I hate being enclosed." She tried to laugh about her phobia, but it was too strong. "I hate being confined. I'd camp out if it weren't so cold now. Maybe I should move south to start over." Only she didn't have enough money to move anywhere for a while. Unless she hitchhiked or something.

"We'll find you outdoor work. Even in the winter months. Maybe at one of the ski resorts?"

"Until they open, what do I do? And that's seasonal work. I need something permanent." She glanced around. Had the place become more crowded? She began to get that edgy feeling—like she was being hemmed in. It reminded her of the same trapped feeling she had when that guard had beaten her so severely. She forced the memory away, took a deep breath.

"Are you all right?" he asked, concern etched on his face.

"I will be," she vowed. If she was ever going to have a normal life, she had to get over her fear of enclosed places, and of crowds. There was plenty of room around her. No one was pushing or shoving. She had plenty of air.

Jared reached out and covered her fist with his warm hand. Shocked, she stared at their hands. Susannah hadn't even known she had clenched her fists. Slowly she forced the muscles to relax. Jared's palm was warm, his fingers soothing. Something seemed to melt inside and the imminent panic began to fade.

"Claustrophobic?" he hazarded a guess.

She nodded. Made so much worse by being in prison.

Slowly his fingers rubbed against the back of her hand, until she opened it and he gripped her hand in his, squeezing gently then letting go.

"We can ask to have our breakfast on the patio, if you like," he said.

She looked through the large windows and saw the forlorn tables puddled with rain, the umbrellas furled.

She almost laughed. "Wouldn't our waitress love that. No, I'm fine." She smiled at him, oddly touched by his gesture. It was cold and damp, not to mention the steady rain, and yet she knew he'd meant the suggestion. She took another deep breath.

"Actually, I need to concentrate on something else, try to forget I'm here. Crowds, enclosed spaces…" She shrugged, maybe she wasn't meant for urban living.

"Once you have a job, you'll need a place to stay. Any ideas where you'd like to live?"

"Only where I don't want to," she said. "I don't want to go anywhere near the apartment Shawn and I lived in. Too many memories, both good and bad." They'd been so happy.

Then Timothy had ended it, for both of them.

"What do you like—glass and steel, old brownstones, or rustic?"

She thought a moment. Glancing out the windows, she sighed. "We live right at the edge of the Rocky Mountains, yet look at all this urban sprawl. I'd love to live with trees, and maybe a creek or something."

"You weren't kidding about camping?"

She smiled at that, starting to feel at ease for the first time around Jared. He watched her constantly, as if he found her the most fascinating person on the planet.

Or was he still suspicious of her? The thought startled her.

"What?" he asked.

"You don't think I killed anyone, do you?"

He shook his head.

"I didn't kill anyone. I said that so much I never

thought anyone would believe me. But you're always watching me. I wondered if you were still speculating if I had done it after all.''

He glanced away, then met her eyes. "I'm having a hard time seeing the young girl at the trial in you today.''

"I was young and naive, wasn't I?''

"Or trusting and in completely over your head.''

Breakfast arrived and for a moment conversation was suspended as they both began to eat. Jared's cell phone rang and he answered. Pulling out a small notebook from his pocket, he jotted down a name, address and phone number then thanked his caller and disconnected.

He tore out the page and handed it to Susannah.

"My secretary has been working on this since I called her earlier. She's found a wholesale nursery that has a possible opening. It's on the west side of town, on a major bus route. If you like, you can call and make an appointment for an interview. If they can see you right away, I'll drive you over.''

"You don't have to do that.'' Her heart skipped a beat. A possible job? In a field she'd grown to love? Surely her luck hadn't changed that much.

"I owe you.''

She wanted to refuse, to tell him she didn't need him or anyone. But it was raining. And a ride in a dry, warm car would be welcomed. Besides he *did* owe her. She'd take him up on the offer.

JARED DROVE her to the interview, waiting in the parking lot while she went inside. He called Rose, while he waited.

"Steve is hopping mad, boss. He wants to know where you are," she said. "I thought you were just going to breakfast. How much are you two eating?"

"We finished a while ago. I drove Susannah to that interview. Tell Steve I'm home sick."

"I tried that, but he doesn't buy it. He's had his secretary call you every half hour trying to reach you. I changed that meeting with Hoffman, and rescheduled all the other appointments you had this morning. Should I clear the entire day?"

"Where is there an inexpensive apartment complex that's safe, and has a lot of green space?" he asked instead of answering her question.

There was silence on the other end for a moment. "Jared, aren't you getting in too deep here? I'm as sorry as the next person about what happened to Susannah Chapman, but you don't owe her the rest of your life."

Why did it feel as if he did? "Just a couple of things to help her get started. If you don't know of any apartments, I'll ask around."

"She might want to try Sunset View Terrace. Fancy name for cheap apartments, but they're on the edge of the green belt on the north side of town. Old as the hills, as I remember, but inexpensive, and I think some units come furnished. I know, I know—check it out."

"You're a gem."

"Remember that at raise time. Watch out for Steve when you finally get here."

Jared knew his boss would have a fit if he knew the extent to which Jared was involved with Susannah. He'd been told to keep a low profile and stay away from reporters. But Steve Johnson didn't share the same feeling of guilt that Jared did.

The rain continued to drizzle. Jared pulled some papers from his briefcase, but couldn't concentrate. He kept thinking about Susannah's child.

He called Rose again and asked her to arrange a meeting between him and one of the family law judges. Criminal law was his area of expertise. He needed some clear-cut answers from an expert in family law before he could proceed.

The door to the warehouse opened just about the time the rain stopped. Susannah almost danced down the sidewalk. She smiled so radiantly it didn't matter that the day was dreary and cold, Jared felt a lick of warmth.

She flung open the door and hopped into the car. "I got the job! I start tomorrow and it pays more than I expected."

"Congratulations."

"I appreciate your help. I don't think I would ever have gotten it otherwise. I'll be working outside most of the time, or in the warehouse. That big building over there. They're already getting ready for spring, planting bulbs, filling orders to ship them, winterizing some of their stock. And they plan to have a Christmas tree farm starting next month here in the parking lot, so I'll be helping with that.''

He enjoyed seeing her so animated. It was as she should have been all her life, if he and Michael hadn't turned it upside down.

''Where to now?'' he asked, starting the engine.

''Just take me back to the motel. I have a list of things to buy for work, sturdy work shoes, warm socks, rain gear, warm clothes.'' She fell silent and Jared glanced over. She was studying the list. From the brief glimpse he got, it was long. Would she have enough money for everything and still cover the motel rates until the first payday?

His cell rang again.

''Walker.''

''Me, boss,'' Rose said. ''I found out more about those apartments, but Ron was just in. And get this. His niece is a student at the university, taking a leave of absence because she broke her leg falling down some stairs. She's off to Wisconsin where her folks live until after the holidays. She hopes to be back in time for the next session. She wants to have someone housesit her place and take care of her cat. It's furnished, and all. Student stuff, I'm sure, but the price is right—zilch, and the cat. What do you think?''

He glanced at his passenger. ''Ask her yourself,'' he said. He held the phone out to Susannah.

''For me?'' she asked.

He nodded.

He hoped she'd take the place. At least this didn't come from him. She'd have no reason to feel beholden. He didn't want that at all.

SUSANNAH WAS ASTONISHED when she heard the offer of an apartment.

"Does the girl know who I am?" she asked Jared's secretary.

"Her uncle does. He's the one who suggested it. You can stop by later and visit with her if you like. She's still in the hospital. Her parents are arriving tomorrow and she'll be heading for Wisconsin. Ron's been running by each day to check on the cat."

"I'd love to watch it until she gets back. Are you sure there's no rent?" What would it mean to have two months rent-free? She could save up her money and be ready to find a place she'd like by the time the girl returned for school.

"No rent. But lavish attention on the cat."

"Give me the information on how to reach her. If she says it's okay after we meet, then yes. I really appreciate this."

Susannah handed Jared the phone after she'd jotted down the directions to the hospital, still dazed. She couldn't believe this turn of events. Maybe life was going to get better every day from now on. Cynically she didn't believe it. But maybe.

CHAPTER SEVEN

SUSANNAH HAD all her things packed. She had to put most of her new clothes back in the store bags she'd brought them home in, but at least she had everything ready to go. Jared Walker was once again giving her a lift.

After today, however, she didn't expect to see him again. She could manage on her own. She wasn't some helpless waif, though he almost acted as if she were. Guilt on his part, she knew. But she was on her way now. He owed her nothing more.

She'd started her job at the garden center and knew she would enjoy working for Pete Talridge. Being outside most of the day was a bonus—even if the temperature was low.

Her meeting with Christine of the broken leg had gone well. Her apartment and cat were now in Susannah's care. Cocoa, the dark tabby she was to watch, was a love. She had never had a pet before, but she thought she'd enjoy having the company.

She checked her watch, a new purchase along with the clothes. She hadn't needed one in prison. Right on time she heard the knock at the door.

Opening it, Susannah stared in surprise. Jared wore

dark cords, a dark sweater and leather jacket. Quite a change from the suits she was used to seeing. Beside him stood a little boy—Eric.

"Ready?" Jared asked.

Susannah nodded, her eyes on the child.

"Eric, this is the lady I was telling you about, Susannah Chapman. Susannah, my son, Eric."

She heard the pride in his voice as she smiled in greeting.

"It's nice to meet you, Eric." She looked up at Jared. "I didn't realize you'd have your son. If this is inconvenient, I can get a cab."

"Not at all. Eric and I spend the weekends together, so where I go, he goes. We're ready to help you move," Jared said.

In no time Eric and Jared had put all her bags and boxes in the trunk of the car.

Susannah left the motel without a backward look. She was starting her new life and didn't need reminders of the immediate past.

"Do you have any pets?" she asked Eric during the drive.

He shook his head.

"I don't either, but I'm going to babysit a cat. What do you think of that?" she asked.

He giggled. "Cats don't get babysitters," he said.

"This one does. I've met him and he's really cute. And affectionate."

As the morning progressed, Susannah was glad that Eric had accompanied them. He explored the apartment, played with Cocoa and chattered constantly. It made dealing with Jared less awkward.

It didn't take long to unload her things, put them away and attend to the cat. Now what? she wondered, as the two Walkers didn't seem inclined to budge an inch from her sofa.

"All done?" Jared asked when she reentered the small living room. The entire apartment was tiny. For a college kid it was perfect. Not so for Susannah. The space was too cramped for comfort. Fortunately, there was a small balcony off the living room that afforded a terrific view. If the apartment began to close in on her, she could stand on the balcony and feel the freedom.

"Yes. Thank you again for all your help," she said politely.

"Come with us today. We're going to the zoo, then to a pizza parlor for dinner."

"I don't think…"

"Can Cocoa come, too, Daddy?" Eric piped up.

"No, he's an indoor cat. He stays here and guards the apartment when Susannah is gone," Jared said. He met her gaze. "Come and enjoy the day with us."

"You don't have to ask me. I'm perfectly capable of being on my own," she said. A part of her longed for the normalcy of visiting the zoo, of sharing a meal with others. But another part of her wanted to distance herself from Jared. She was growing too dependent on him and his help.

And she was already charmed by Eric, which could be dangerous.

"If you won't come with us, we'll just stay here," Jared said, sitting back on the sofa.

"Just stay here," Eric repeated, sitting beside his father and crossing his arms over his chest in imitation.

"Okay, I'll go," Susannah said, giving in to the yearning. What would one day hurt? She would enjoy herself and then say goodbye.

The day was windy but sunny, normal for early November. Snow blanketed the Front Range, but so far hadn't fallen on Denver.

The zoo was packed, and each exhibit had a healthy number of spectators vying for space to watch the animals. Susannah stayed on the perimeter of any group, not wanting to spoil the day with a claustrophobic attack. She expected Eric to like the monkeys best, but he preferred the giant Komodo dragon. He asked Jared a hundred questions about the creature. Susannah listened to his answers, surprised he seemed to know so much about the animal.

He looked at her and winked, then nodded toward a display placard which listed facts about the dragon.

They ate hot dogs and sodas, wandered around until the afternoon waned and the breeze turned downright cold.

"We'll head back to my place until time for dinner," Jared said when they were in the warmth of the car.

"Can I show Susannah my room, Daddy?" Eric asked from his seat in the back.

"I'm sure she would love to see your room," Jared responded.

Susannah looked back at the little boy. "I would indeed. So you have a room at your daddy's place and one at your mommy's?"

"Uh-huh. But I like the one at Daddy's best. I can do what I want there. Mommy always says pick up after myself and don't take out more than one toy at a time."

Susannah looked at Jared. "And you don't make him pick up his toys?"

"Only when he leaves."

"I gots a train, too," Eric said. "It goes round and round and I can make it go really fast, or really slow."

"Sounds like you have a lot to show me," she said. She had been around young children while student teaching, and for a moment she wished she could teach. Being with the kids had been the best part and she missed it.

Jared's apartment complex utilized top security. There were buttons to push to get the car parked, then a card to insert into the elevator. Another stop in the lobby under the scrutiny of a guard to switch to another elevator, this one servicing the floors above. His apartment was on one of the upper stories of the tall building.

Susannah was already having trouble by the time

the elevator reached his floor. She quickly stepped out of the small box and tried to breathe normally. Her skin felt clammy, her hands damp. She still had to go back down. Coming here had been a mistake.

Jared touched her shoulder and pointed down the hall. "That way."

She shrank back, then tried to cover the motion by heading quickly in the direction he indicated. He had done nothing but be kind. He was not some testosterone-ladened bully showing off for other guards. He had never given her any indication he'd physically hurt her.

But the old fears refused to leave. Would she always expect the worst?

Expensive was the first word to come to mind when she entered his apartment. Lots of leather furnishings, chrome and glass, everything in black and silver. A man's home, no doubt about it.

"Come with me, Susannah," Eric said, tugging on her hand. "My room is this way."

"Let her get her jacket off first," Jared said.

"I want her to see my room!" Eric said, temper rising.

"When she gets her jacket off," Jared replied.

"Is your room going to disappear if we don't get there right away?" she teased, amused by his impatience. Jared seemed to take it in stride. Obviously not the first time he'd dealt with a cranky child.

"No, but I want you to see it now."

Susannah relinquished her jacket to Jared and followed Eric to his room.

The room was perfect for a small boy. And from what Susannah could see, Jared had not denied his son a single toy, it seemed. The train was set up on the floor near the windows. There were shelves loaded with action figures, cars, trucks, a football and a soccer ball. Near the bed was a bookcase full of books, several looking torn, tattered and much-loved.

"It's a wonderful room," Susannah said. After Eric had shown her how the train ran, he asked her to read him a story, and she couldn't refuse.

He snuggled right up against her when she settled against the headboard of his bed. She took the books he handed her and began to read the first one. She'd never done this before. For a moment the book blurred. Did her daughter's mother snuggle with her and read to her?

Jared appeared in the doorway, studying the scene for a long moment.

Susannah looked up. "Did you want something?" she asked.

"I wondered if you two wanted something to drink. Hot chocolate maybe?"

"Yes!" Eric called from his spot. "Can we have it in here?"

"You know we don't bring food or drinks here," Jared said.

Eric frowned and looked up at Susannah. "I thought he might let you, 'cause you're company."

"Ah, but I follow the rules just like anyone else," she said.

"I'll call you two when the drinks are ready," he said.

Susannah smiled at Eric, her heart blossoming. She'd been freed from prison, had started her new life, but until this very moment, she had not felt happiness.

But she was happy, she realized. For this moment, with this child, she was happy.

Jared called them from the dining area when the hot chocolate was ready. He'd put miniature marshmallows on the top. Eric obviously knew the drill—he climbed up on his chair and opened a napkin before carefully taking the hot beverage.

"I cooled his down with milk, but yours is hot," he said, setting a mug before Susannah.

"This is a treat," she said, sitting opposite Jared. She watched Eric scoop out some of the gooey, melted marshmallows. Watching him was easier than looking at Jared. She felt more at ease around the child than his sexy father.

She blinked. Where had that thought come from? Jared wasn't sexy. He was one of the men who had been instrumental in sending her to prison.

She pushed the mug away and rose.

"I have to leave," she said.

"Why?" He was staring at her.

"I just do. Thanks for everything."

"But we didn't eat pizza yet," Eric said, distressed.

"I know but I can't stay—" Before Susannah could finish her sentence a knock sounded at the door.

Jared went to answer it.

"Eric left his teddy bear behind. I know how he likes it when he goes to bed," a woman said as she entered the apartment.

The ex-wife, Susannah surmised.

She was stunning, tall and slender. Her auburn hair was styled to emphasize her beauty. The trendy pants and sweater were topped by a short suede coat that had to have cost a mint.

Noelle, that was what Jared had said her name was. A pretty name for a beautiful woman.

Susannah felt a spurt of envy as she stood by the table, watching Eric's parents. They made a beautiful couple. What had gone wrong in their marriage?

Noelle realized Susannah was in the room at that moment.

"What's going on?" she asked, advancing into the dining area. "Who are you?"

"Susannah Chapman," Susannah replied.

Noelle spun around. "Jared, I won't have you expose my son to that woman. You're supposed to be spending time with Eric, not entertaining riffraff. If this is how you spend your weekends with my son, I'm taking him home."

"No, Mommy, I don't want to go. I want to stay for pizza," Eric said. "Daddy said we can go for pizza and it's my favorite."

"Hold on, Noelle. You know I'm entitled to have

Eric on weekends. And what we do on our time is our business. I'll bring him home tomorrow as planned,'' Jared said evenly.

"Not if you plan to consort with that…that ex-con. I do not wish to have Eric exposed to such people. He's just a little boy.''

"No, Mommy! I want to stay!'' Eric yelled, jumping down from the table and running to his room.

"Cut the theatrics, Noelle. Now you've gotten Eric upset. Susannah was exonerated, remember? And I'm certainly entitled to introduce my son to anyone I see fit.''

"Just because the conviction was overturned, doesn't mean anyone can instantly erase eight years in prison with the kind of people who are there. Who knows what habits she picked up. Or what kind of revenge she's plotting against you. You've handed her the perfect weapon with my son.'' She rounded on Susannah. "If you ever come within a mile of Eric again, I'll press charges.''

"Press charges? I've done nothing wrong.'' Susannah couldn't believe what she was hearing. How could the woman even suspect she'd harm a child? Susannah was shocked by the venom in Noelle's tone.

"Stalking. Endangering a child. I'll find something. But Eric will not be used as a pawn for revenge against my husband. I'm sorry you got sent to jail, but it had nothing to do with Eric.'' Noelle stepped back, as if fearful Susannah would strike out.

Jared stepped in between them. "Stop it, Noelle.''

"I have no plans for revenge," Susannah said. "And I would never hurt a child. I was about to leave when you arrived." She really wanted to make a dash for the door and escape, but both Noelle and Jared stood in her way.

"Then don't let me stop you," Noelle said, glaring at her.

"That's enough, Noelle." Jared spun her around, holding her by her shoulders. "Susannah is a guest in my home and you will treat her with respect."

"Oh, wise up, Jared, she's playing you. How could you let her have access to Eric? Or your own place, for that matter? You don't know what she's capable of."

Susannah had had enough. "You don't have to worry about revenge or anything else. I'll just get my jacket and leave." Susannah headed for the closet near the door.

"No," Jared said. "Stay."

"What?" Noelle was clearly taken aback. She recovered quickly, leaning toward Jared, anger evident in her face. "I will not let my child stay and be exposed to…to whatever evil she has in mind."

"Dammit, Noelle, she was innocent. Get that into your head."

"He's in my custody and I'm taking him home. You can play savior, but not at the risk of my son!"

Five minutes later, Noelle and a tearful, unhappy Eric were gone. Susannah hadn't moved, still stunned by the scene that had just played out. Now she watched Jared warily. Did he believe what Noelle had said—that she was out for some kind of revenge?

"I'm sorry for causing trouble. I should never have come here." She just wanted to get her jacket and leave.

"Of course you should have come, and you didn't cause any trouble, Noelle did," he said. "She over-reacted, that's all. If you knew her better, you'd know she has always had a bent toward the dramatic."

"Well, I'll be on my way, now." She edged around the room, keeping as much distance between them as she could. His anger still simmered. She didn't want it focused on her.

"You and I can still go out for pizza," Jared said.

"I'll just head back to my new apartment. Cocoa is probably wondering where I am."

He looked at her. Susannah could see the turmoil in his eyes. "Have dinner with me," he said softly. "Please."

Every instinct urged her to flee. But the appeal in his eyes held her.

"I'm not after revenge—at least not against you," she said. "Timothy might be a different story."

"I never thought you were."

"And I would never hurt a child."

"I know that. If Noelle would think for a moment, she'd know that as well. There's history between us, and a power play in motion. She wants something she can't have and is doing all she can to fight for it. Don't let her get to you."

"She called you her husband. I thought you said you were divorced."

"We were divorced eighteen months ago. She has trouble remembering that sometimes. You have no other plans. We can still salvage the evening. Stay and have dinner with me."

"At a pizza place?"

"Do you want to eat somewhere else?"

She shook her head. She was so tempted. It had been years since she'd had thick, hot pizza with everything on it. Could she risk spending more time with this disturbing man? She didn't want to return to her apartment, hiding away like she didn't have a right to do anything she wanted. She had finally been freed. Time she lived the way she wanted.

He held out his hand. She needed to step closer to take it. Was this a test of some kind? Staring at his hand, her heart sped up. Was he asking for more than dinner? Was he offering friendship? Could two people with the history they had between them become friends?

She doubted it. She would never forget the relentless cross-examination from Michael Denning, the support offered him by his team—of which Jared had been a member.

A junior member, she reminded herself.

The past was over, nothing could change it. She had choices to make, and one was what to do about the man who was trying so hard to make up for something that could never be made up.

Slowly she took that step and another, reached out and placed her hand in his. He tightened his fingers against hers, and drew her even closer.

"Eric was having a great time today. I'm sorry it got interrupted. We'll have to plan something for another weekend," he said.

"It's not your fault." She didn't know how to extricate her hand without making a big deal of it, so she left it in his. It actually felt sort of good to have a connection with someone. It had been so long since anyone had touched her, held her. For the first time since that guard had beaten her, she felt no flash of fear being so close to a man.

"What do you like on your pizza?" he asked.

"Everything!"

AS WOULD BE EXPECTED on a Saturday night, the pizza parlor was jammed. Taking a step inside, Susannah almost turned and ran. Too many people, too much noise.

Jared was right behind her. He put his hands on her shoulders. She tensed.

"Relax, I'm not going to hurt you," he said in her ear. Gently he propelled her toward the order counter. "Some day you'll have to tell me why you don't like being touched."

She tried to quell the fears that churned. Could she do this or not? She wanted a normal life. She refused to be ruled by fear.

After they ordered, he carried a pitcher of soda and

two glasses to a spot at the end of a long table with benches on either side. He sat opposite her, leaving a little space between him and the man already seated on the long bench.

"You okay?" he asked.

She sat on the edge of the bench, putting as much room as she could between herself and the woman seated next to her, who was laughing at her companion and enjoying the pizza they shared. Susannah wanted that kind of relaxation.

She nodded, reaching out to pour the drinks. It gave her something to do. She wished she could relax.

"Have they found Timothy yet?" she asked.

"The San Francisco police have given the search a top priority. He vacated the apartment he'd been living in, but after questioning his friends, several leads have surfaced. They predict they'll catch him before long. The bank account he opened under his assumed name has been frozen, so money will become an issue. His car was impounded, and his known friends alerted about the reason for the questioning. Sooner or later, he'll turn up."

"He didn't eight years ago," she said.

"We weren't looking for him then."

"Who was the murdered man, do you know?"

"Not a clue. But we've been searching missing person reports from the time of the murder—none match the victim's description."

"Can't something be done to hurry the process?"

"I believe the police are doing all they can to find him."

She brooded for a moment. If only someone had searched for him eight years ago, her life would have been so different.

"I still want to see him when he's caught. He'll be brought back here, right?" she asked.

"Yes. The extradition paperwork has already been started. I can't guarantee you'll get to see him, though."

"Yes, you can. You make sure I do. You owe me that much." She would not be shunted aside. The entire state of Colorado owed her at least that much.

"Steve Johnson has the final say," Jared said.

"I've been watching the news some evenings. They're still harping on the conviction of an innocent person. My release has been a major part of the election grandstanding for Johnson, don't you think? But I haven't heard your name mentioned. Maybe I should clue people in to who really opened up the case."

"Have you been contacted by the media?" Jared asked.

"They don't know where I am." She narrowed her eyes as she looked at him. "But I could change all that if I don't get to see Timothy."

"Threats?" he said mildly.

Susannah was a bit annoyed he didn't seem more upset. How to convince him she *had* to see Timothy. She'd never have a normal life if she didn't get some closure. And she wanted more than anything to know why he'd done the crime, and let her take the punishment.

"Promises," she said.

"I'll do my best," Jared said.

THEY HAD JUST BEGUN to eat their pizza a few minutes later when a commotion in the entryway made Susannah turn around. A brilliant flash startled her. In seconds, two men pushed through the restaurant crowd to the end of their table, one snapping pictures like crazy, the other shoving a microphone in front of her face.

"Susannah Chapman, right? How does it feel to be free after so long? What are your plans now that you're out?" He looked at Jared, then did a double take. "Assistant District Attorney Walker? What are you doing here?" He looked back and gestured to his partner to get photos of the both of them.

"Not now," Jared said, rising.

"Consorting with the enemy?" the reporter asked her. "What have you been doing since you got out? My readers would love to have the inside scoop. Tell me what it's like on the outside after so long. What was your first indulgence?"

Jared came around the table, brushed the obnoxious reporter aside and reached for Susannah's arm.

She was too stunned to resist. Snatching her jacket at the last moment, she clung to Jared as they left the restaurant, dodging the reporter and his photographer.

Jared kept repeating no comment, but Susannah didn't even have the voice to say that. She felt like she was in some surreal nightmare. The flashing lights blinded her, the constant stream of questions confused her. She just wanted to be left alone.

Finally they reached Jared's car. He put her inside and locked the door before closing it behind her. Turning, he addressed the reporter once again before hurrying to his side and getting in.

The flashes continued as he drove away.

"Gee, dinner with you is certainly exciting," she said a couple of minutes later, still feeling shaken. "How did they find us?"

"My guess would be Noelle. She knew from Eric's tantrum we were planning on pizza. She knows enough of my routine to be able to guess where we'd go. I'm sure she alerted the media. We were lucky there was only one reporter, not a whole crew from a TV station."

Susannah looked over her shoulder. "No one is following us, right?"

"No."

"I don't want to go through that again. If they found my new apartment, I'd be pestered to death." The mere thought of it caused her stomach to clench. Her earlier threats to Jared would be revealed as the bluff they were. She could never go to the media to stir things up.

"Your location is safe. I'm sorry our dinner got

interrupted. Want to go back to my place and order in?''

"No, thank you. I just want to go home." She'd had enough "normalcy" for one day. Closing herself in the apartment and having only a cat for company sounded perfect at this moment.

They arrived at her building a short time later.

"Are you going to be all right?" Jared asked as he pulled the car to the curb.

"Yes." She turned to him. "I enjoyed today. Most of it, anyway. Thank you for letting me meet your son. He's darling. You are blessed."

"I'll call you tomorrow," Jared said when she opened her door.

"Please don't. I think you've done more than needed to help me get established again. I appreciate all you've done, but I've got to make it on my own." She quickly slid out. "Goodbye, Jared."

Before she changed her mind, she hurried into the apartment building.

CHAPTER EIGHT

JARED COULD HAVE wrung Noelle's neck. He was furious with her for her actions on Saturday—both the display at his apartment and for sending the reporters to the restaurant. Seems as if her anger over the divorce had not dissipated since it became final. If this was her way to get him back, he was in for a hard time. And not only him, but Susannah as well.

The newspaper report on Sunday was worse than Jared had feared. Several photos of him and Susannah were splashed across the lifestyle page, complete with speculation about their relationship. Steve would have a fit. They were two days before the election. If this adversely affected the polls, the man would be furious.

When Jared showed up at work on Monday, Rose was already there, looking upset.

"Oh, boss, trouble brewing," she said.

"I expected as much. Steve on the warpath?"

"And some. I'd stay out of his way if I were you."

He had scarcely hung up his jacket when Steve strode into his office.

"Have you lost your marbles?" he asked, tossing down a copy of Sunday's paper. "Tomorrow is the election. How does this make our office look? Damn stupid if you ask me. Is there something going on between you and Susannah Chapman?''

"I took her to pizza. What's wrong with that?'' Jared asked.

"Everything. You were on the team that prosecuted her. You were instrumental in getting her released. Cozying up to her now, smacks of some kind of conspiracy or something.''

"No one but you and a couple of others know I had anything to do with her release,'' Jared said. He suspected what was coming. Maybe it was no more than he deserved for fouling up so badly eight years ago.

"You stay away from her, hear me, Jared? I don't want you to even be on the same street as her. She was wrongfully convicted. Now she's released. The sooner the public forgets the blot on this office, the better. Get me?''

"The woman lost eight years of her life. I'm not going to sit by and ignore that if I can help her get back on track,'' Jared argued.

"Taking her to dinner isn't getting her back on track. If you want to be some do-gooder behind the scenes, that's fine, but in public, you stay away from her!''

Jared held on to his temper by a thread. He and Steve both knew what he did on his own time was his own business. But for the sake of harmony in the office, he wouldn't argue the point at this juncture.

Neither would he agree to it, however. He wanted to see Susannah again.

A few moments after Steve left, Jared moved from the window and sat down, staring at the work on his desk. He'd been a valued member of the district attorney's office since he started nine years ago. He had a high conviction rate, strong work ethics and integrity to know when to right a wrong.

But all Steve was interested in was publicity on the eve of the election. He wasn't the one who had been in the wrong. He wasn't the one who wanted to make restitution in any way he could.

If his boss learned of his plan to try and find Susannah's daughter, Steve would really go nuts—he might go as far as to threaten Jared's job.

"Judge Creighton called last Friday. He can see you tomorrow morning, if you still want," Rose said, appearing in the doorway.

Perfect. Judge Creighton was one of the leading family court judges in Denver. He'd been on the bench for a couple of decades. If anyone knew the ins and outs, it would be him.

"I do. What time?" He wouldn't take anyone into his confidence about what he was doing. If it amounted to nothing, no one's hopes would be raised.

Rose gave him the information. She paused before turning and smiled. "So do I vote yes for our illustrious incumbent D.A., or for his rival?"

"Vote your conscience," Jared said. Right now he felt hard pressed to be supportive.

SUSANNAH LOVED her new job. The only drawback was the commute. The first two mornings she had gotten off the bus long before her stop as the crush of people had panic flaring. She'd rather walk than be in that pack. Allowing plenty of time, she made sure she would not be late. She didn't want to risk jeopardizing this new position.

It was ideal. Pete Talridge gave her certain responsibilities, then let her go. He didn't hang over her shoulder, tell her how to do the job, or demand an accounting of every action. He was a short, balding man, seriously overweight, with an unlit cigar constantly in the left corner of his mouth. But the nursery was well run, and the other employees seemed content to work there.

The weather was cold, but clear. With her new warm clothes, she felt ready to tackle anything. Always asking questions, she focused on quickly learning all she could about bulbs and planting techniques. Pete had commented that when spring came and people began planting vegetable gardens he could use her expertise in advising them.

Pete had one of the other women working there take Susannah under her wing and teach her the ropes. Eva Reynolds took her job training seriously, but had plenty of time to talk.

Only a year or so older than Susannah, Eva was divorced and playing the field, as she told her. "No sense in limiting my opportunities. The next time I marry, I plan to stay married. So I need to make sure all the bachelors in Denver have an equal opportunity.''

Susannah laughed when Eva told her that. It was nice to have another woman to talk with. She really missed Marissa.

From the first, Eva took her coffee breaks with Susannah. She also tried to talk Susannah into going out to a bar with her, but Susannah wasn't ready for that step yet. Susannah didn't say much about her ordeal. Eva was aware of the circumstances, and sympathetic, but pragmatic. Never questioning.

''It's behind you. Look forward. There's a lot Denver and its men have to offer,'' she said.

Susannah laughed. It was late afternoon, the skies were laden with dark clouds. Rain was expected. She just hoped it held off until she reached home. Bad weather would make the bus even more crowded than normal.

''I'm not ready to start dating,'' she said.

''What about that hunk in the paper yesterday?'' Eva asked.

''What are you talking about?'' Susannah didn't subscribe to a paper. She had begun to avoid the news on TV after seeing her story reported more times than she cared to.

''Didn't you see it in the lifestyle section? You and some gorgeous man dodging reporters—Jared Walker. Ring a bell?'' Eva said. ''I wish I'd brought the paper today.''

Susannah looked at her in dismay. "Our pictures were in the paper?"

"Newsworthy, I guess. The guy who sent you up, now taking you to dinner. There was a lot of speculation and innuendoes, but I mostly focused on the photos. That guy's hot!"

"Oh," Susannah groaned. "I'm trying to keep a low profile. I don't want reporters finding me. They were awful at the courthouse when I got released. Like sharks circling."

"You're news, honey. They all want the scoop."

"There is no scoop. I just want to be left alone."

"Don't worry, no one here would blow the whistle. But I want the skinny on the guy in the picture," Eva said.

"We went to the zoo with his little boy on Saturday, then had dinner at a pizza place. No big deal." But it had been a wonderful day—despite Noelle and the reporter.

"Not my idea of a hot date, but hey, it takes all kinds," Eva said, lifting her mug for another sip.

"It wasn't a date," Susannah protested.

"Oh. What do you call it?" Eva asked, her eyes amused.

"An outing. He just invited me along."

"Why?"

Susannah looked at her new friend. "I guess he felt sorry for me. Or it's his idea of atonement. He's really trying hard to make things better."

"Guilt, of course. Why not? He screwed up royally."

"He wasn't the lead prosecutor, just one of the flunkies at the table." Susannah didn't know why she had to defend Jared, but she wanted Eva to understand. Michael Denning was the man behind the conviction, not Jared.

Eva studied her for a moment. "Don't fall for the guy if those are his motives. Once he feels the debt is paid, he'll move on."

"I'm not falling for anyone. And as far as I'm concerned, I don't care if I never see him again. He helped me find this job, found me a temporary place to live. The debt is wiped clean."

"Ha, eight years of your life is gone, that's a huge debt. A couple of favors don't wipe it out."

"Well, he doesn't have to do anything for me from now on. Break is over, I have work to do."

Susannah rose and tossed out her foam cup and headed back to work, grateful for the excuse to escape Eva's analysis of the situation.

Susannah knew Jared had only wanted to help as a way to repay the wrong. There was nothing more to his offers of friendship. Now that she was established, he had no reason to see her again.

She hoped the photos in the paper didn't revive the feeding frenzy of the reporters and send them searching after her. She'd managed to avoid any contact once she'd left the jail. She wanted to keep it that way.

When Susannah reached home that night, she sat down to write Marissa, telling her everything that had happened since her release. She included her new address, knowing Marissa would write as soon as she could. She missed her friend. She told her about Eva and her new job, but skipped over most of the help Jared had given her. She wasn't quite sure why, except Marissa was too cynical to accept he'd helped for altruistic reasons, and Susannah didn't want to get a tirade back from her friend.

WEDNESDAY when Susannah arrived at work, Eva joined her. "Did you see the election results? The incumbent D.A. won another four years. They're saying he got it so easily because of your release. Now he's known as some crusader for justice."

"He had little to do with it. Jared Walker found new evidence, started the investigation, pushed to have the conviction overturned. The district attorney just used his position to take the credit," Susannah said.

"I also notice the D.A. isn't doing anything to help you since you got out. Maybe you should have gone on record with reporters, let the citizens of Denver know he wasn't the one who is responsible."

"Never." The last thing Susannah wanted was to get involved in such a thing. She was free, she was starting over. That was enough.

"Okay, your call. I found the coolest bar. Actually Harlan took me there," Eva said.

"Harlan?" Susannah had trouble keeping track of all the men Eva talked about.

"A guy I met Friday when I was out with Brett. Anyway, we should go on Friday."

"I don't think so."

"When, then?" Eva asked seriously.

Susannah shrugged. "I'm just getting used to being on my own. I feel I'm in a halfway situation. The apartment isn't really mine, I'm just house-sitting for a couple of months. This job seems perfect, but I'm afraid to trust in anything these days. I could get fired tomorrow."

"That's unlikely. You've picked up everything really quickly, and know a lot more about vegetables than I do and I've been here four years. Though I can understand your reluctance to join the social scene, you have to get out sometime."

"Maybe, when things are more settled."

"Ah, any word on finding Timothy Winters?"

"Jared said there are several law enforcement agencies looking for him. But so far he hasn't turned up." Of course that was old news, she hadn't spoken to him for several days. But surely she would have heard from him if Timothy had been located.

"Which means squat. They should be shot for screwing up your trial so badly."

She sipped her hot chocolate, warming her fingers against the mug. "I just hope they let me talk to Timothy when they find him."

"If the cops find him. They didn't do so good eight years ago," Eva said.

"They weren't looking for him eight years ago. They were so sure I'd blown his face off. It never occurred to anyone that Timothy might be hiding somewhere."

"Morbid. Let's talk about something else. If you don't want to go out on Friday, want to go shopping with me on Saturday? We get paid this week, remember? So let's go blow it on some fancy clothes."

Susannah smiled at the thought. How long had it been since she'd gone shopping with a friend? Sometime in college, she thought.

She had to watch her money more carefully than Eva appeared to, but it would be fun to see what was out there.

"You're on. When and where?"

"At ten, Sixteenth Street Mall. We'll shop up one side, have lunch, then do the other side," Eva said, her eyes sparkling with excitement. "It wouldn't hurt to get your hair styled, either."

"You don't like the chopped-off look?" Susannah said, knowing she hadn't cared in prison what her hair looked like, but now everything was different.

"The short style is cute on you, but your hair needs to be trimmed or shaped or something."

"I'm not out to impress anyone." But even as she said it, Susannah remembered how elegant Noelle Walker had looked, and how dowdy and awkward she'd felt standing in the same room with the woman.

A few dollars spent getting her hair styled would go a long way in making her feel better. Maybe, after she had her makeover, she could see Jared and not feel like some kind of charity case, but feel like a normal woman.

"And makeup," she said. Might as well go whole hog.

Eva nodded. "Then you'll have to go out to show off the new you!"

WHEN SUSANNAH returned from lunch, Pete called her from his office door. She veered in that direction.

"There's a police detective waiting to speak to you," he said.

For a moment, sheer panic flared. Had there been a mistake? Had someone come to arrest her and take her back to prison? She paused, debating whether to try to run or not. She didn't think she could take being incarcerated again. Not after this heady taste of freedom.

"Detective Davis and you can use my office, if you like," Pete said easily.

She nodded, swallowing hard, hoping the fear that almost choked her didn't show. She'd learned in prison to never let them know she was afraid.

"What do you want?" she asked after stepping into Pete's office. Her boss left, closing the door behind him.

"I'm not here to cause you any problems, Ms. Chapman. We're hoping you can help us. Won't you have a seat?'' The detective gestured to one of the utilitarian chairs in the office.

Slowly Susannah went over and sat down.

Once she had, he took the other chair. Opening a notebook, he looked at her. ''Tell me what you can remember about Timothy Winters and any comments he made about California.''

''I told Mr. Walker all I remembered,'' she said, trying to relax when she realized he was here hoping she could help the police, not to send her back to prison.

''Some friend named Sammie was all he related to us,'' the detective said.

''Yes, and mention of Disneyland. I think she lived in the L.A. area. But she could have lived in San Francisco, I guess.''

''Nothing else?''

She shook her head.

''Timothy was a friend of yours here in Denver eight years ago, right?''

''Actually, he was a friend of my fiancé. They'd met at high school when Shawn's family moved to Denver. They'd been friends ever since. I saw him a lot since he hung around Shawn that summer.''

''Know of his other friends here in Denver?''

''A few. Wouldn't his family be a better source?''

''We're asking them as well. He lived in a small house near the university, not at his parents' home,'' the detective continued, referring to his notebook.

''His father had bought it for him before he graduated. But we didn't go there often. Mostly he came to our apartment.''

''Why was that?''

Susannah frowned in thought. Why had Timothy always come over to their place? She only remembered going to his house once that summer. His home had been more spacious than their apartment, separated from neighbors for privacy.

''I don't know,'' she said slowly.

''You stated Timothy Winters was gay, did you know that or merely suspect it?''

''I knew it. He wasn't open, but Shawn was his friend and knew. Shawn told me. We didn't talk about it much, though.'' She shrugged. It was as if she were talking about three people she barely knew.

''So, again, who were some of his other friends?''

She leaned back, trying to remember that last summer. Mostly she recalled the heartbreak of Shawn's death, and the nightmare that followed. It was hard to think about the earlier days, happier days.

''I remember him talking about someone called Todd. But we never met him.''

At the detective's encouraging nod, she continued, ''I think he was someone special, but I didn't know much about him. I did hear Timothy talking to Shawn about him one day. There was also Bob Parrish and Harry Sutto. Mostly Timothy hung around us.''

''No special female friends?''

Susannah shook her head. ''I think that's why

Shawn told me—I asked if we should fix Timothy up with a girl so we could double date.''

''Nothing about San Francisco or what he'd do if he didn't stay in Denver?''

She shook her head again. ''He never talked about leaving. He and Shawn always talked up great plans to set the world on fire.''

''But he was the cause of Shawn Anderson's death,'' the detective said.

''Yes.''

''What happened?''

''Don't you have that in the records?''

''Tell me your version,'' he said.

''Shawn and Timothy had gone out, to visit Harry. I wasn't feeling good, so I stayed home. Apparently they ended up partying until the wee hours. I think Harry had just gotten a big raise where he worked. Then Timothy drove them home, drunk. He crashed the car and Shawn was killed.''

''He was under indictment for DUI,'' the detective said.

Susannah nodded. ''From things he'd said earlier, I thought he might get off with just a slap on the wrist. His family had a lot of clout in Denver.''

''You threatened him at the funeral,'' the detective said.

''I'm not on trial anymore,'' she said.

''Just trying to get the picture.''

''I was upset. It seemed so unfair. Timothy walking around while we were burying Shawn. I couldn't stand it. So, yes, I ranted at him, and even threatened him. But I wouldn't have done anything. Once my anger cooled, I couldn't have done anything.''

''You said he came to see you the night of the murder. Why?''

''To tell me he understood why I was so devastated about Shawn's death. He was upset himself. Shawn had been his best friend. He asked if I had any idea how it hurt to know he'd caused his death.''

''So he made no threats or anything?''

''No, just said he didn't want me so mad at him. Then he left.''

He withdrew a card and held it out toward Susannah. ''If you think of anything that might help our investigation, please let me know. I'm sorry for the miscarriage of justice. We are doing all we can to find the man, Ms. Chapman.''

She took the card, holding back the scathing remarks that hovered on her lips. This man wasn't the investigating officer of eight years ago. Her incarceration wasn't this man's fault.

''If I think of anything else, I'll call you,'' she promised. Especially if it would help locate Timothy Winters.

''Boss, Mrs. Walker is—''

Rose was cut off as the door flew open and Noelle stood on the threshold.

Jared looked up wishing he didn't have to deal with

this situation again, it was getting tiresome. He rose. ''Come in and shut the door.''

''How could you send the police to question me?'' Noelle asked angrily.

''Close the door unless you want the entire office staff to hear you,'' Jared said.

She slammed the door and stalked to his desk, tossing down her purse. ''This whole situation is humiliating. I know nothing about my cousin. I thought he died eight years ago.''

''What are you talking about? The police came to question you about what?''

''As if you didn't know.''

''Calm down, Noelle. I didn't know. But I guess it's not unexpected. They questioned me, and I think they were going to question Susannah Chapman again.''

''Serves her right,'' Noelle said with a wave of her hand.

''You sent the reporters to the pizza parlor Saturday night, didn't you?'' Jared asked. He knew she had, but wanted confirmation.

For a moment she almost smiled. ''Any reason why I shouldn't?''

''No, it's a free country. And as such, I can see whomever I wish. Tell me about the cops.''

''Two detectives came to the house this morning, wanting to know what I knew about Timothy and why I hadn't said anything about his being gay eight years ago. They were most unpleasant.''

"Somehow I doubt that. They're doing their job."

"I thought they did that eight years ago," she said.

"So did we all. They're doing it again now. What did you tell them?" Jared asked patiently. He didn't have time for histrionics today. He bet if the detectives had seen Susannah, she'd be even more upset than Noelle, for entirely different reasons. He wanted to call her, to reassure her if he could. He hadn't spoken with her since Saturday. But that didn't mean he hadn't thought about her constantly.

"I told them nothing. I said I'd need to consult my attorney first," she said.

"Why?"

"Why? To protect myself, of course," she said.

"Against what? You didn't deliberately mislead anyone eight years ago. You didn't withhold any information, did you?"

"But the fact he was gay turned out to be a turning point, right?" she said.

"Did you deliberately withhold the information?"

"Of course not. I didn't know it eight years ago."

"Speculation now is the man who was murdered was Timothy's lover. His fingerprints were found all over the house, bathroom, bedroom, kitchen. Was your cousin seeing anyone that summer? Any special male friend? Did you know of a roommate or something? If you know anything, you need to tell the police. They are not accusing you of anything, only seeking information."

"Oh." She looked deflated. "I don't know anything. I guess I need to call the police back and tell them that.''

''You should have done that to begin with.''

She rallied, reaching to pick up her purse. ''I don't suppose you want to come with me?''

''You don't need me,'' Jared said.

Before she could say anything about always needing him, he changed the subject. ''I'm taking Eric up to the cabin this weekend. I'll pick him up Friday night.''

''You keep him away from criminals,'' she snapped.

''Susannah Chapman is not a criminal. Her record has been expunged. She can go anywhere, do anything she wants. Besides, she's a nice woman. A little shy and uncertain about things, but basically nice.''

Noelle's eyes narrowed. ''You can't be interested in her.''

''Whom I see is no longer your concern. You can rest easy, however. I would never put my son at any risk.''

''I would think it could be construed as a conflict of interest, if you were seeing her,'' Noelle said slowly.

''You and Johnson see alike in that. He was furious after the picture in the paper last Sunday.''

''Fearing for his election, I suspect,'' she murmured.

''Once he was reelected, I was back in his good graces,'' Jared said, still annoyed at the personal turn of the entire situation. He didn't need Noelle or Steve interfering with his life at this point.

She rose and looked lost for a moment. Jared wondered why she couldn't let go. Martin seemed to adore her, and they were well suited. He offered her the kind of life Noelle needed. Why couldn't she see that?

ONCE NOELLE LEFT, Jared returned to his desk. She would do fine with the detectives. But even if she had needed his help, he wouldn't have gone with her.

He'd met with Judge Creighton regarding adoptions. The news hadn't been good. The records were sealed and only a court order could unseal them. Unless Susannah petitioned to have that done, and provided a compelling reason to do so, it wouldn't happen.

He wouldn't suggest it to her unless there was no other way. To get her hopes up when the petition could be denied, was too cruel. He'd find out what he could by other means.

He'd already started by talking to one of the clerks in the records department.

He knew he was violating regulations, but didn't care. If he could give Susannah the assurance her daughter was all right, it would be worth the risk. He couldn't imagine giving up Eric and not knowing anything about him for the rest of his life. Reassurance was all she was asking. He'd do what he could to provide it—to hell with the rules.

CHAPTER NINE

MIDAFTERNOON on Saturday, Susannah hefted her packages and stepped from the bus. She was only a block from her apartment. Which was a good thing, she thought, shifting the heavy shopping bag. With all she had bought, she could hardly carry everything.

Eva had offered to bring her home, but Susannah knew her building was out of her friend's way, so she had declined the offer.

The wind blew from the west, cold and dry. The sun shone overhead, but didn't contribute much warmth. If the weather changed, it was cold enough to snow.

She slowed her pace when she drew near her apartment building. Jared and Eric were on the sidewalk, having a serious discussion. What were they doing here? she wondered, her heart skipping a beat despite her vow to have nothing further to do with them after last weekend.

Eric saw her first and dodged around his dad, running toward her. Her heart lifted at the joy in his face.

"Hi, Susannah. We've been waiting and waiting. Did you know you have a song? We learned it in kindergarten and I know all the words!"

"Hi, yourself, Eric. You know all the words? Good for you."

He reached out and manfully took one of the shopping bags, struggling to hold it off the sidewalk as he walked along beside her.

Jared had turned when Eric dashed away, but he moved more slowly toward her, as if unsure of his welcome.

His gaze was assessing, and Susannah's spirits rose. The new hairstyle was flattering, the makeup subtle, but it gave her a lot more confidence than she'd started out with this morning.

"No need to ask where you've been," Jared said when he reached her. He reached out to lift two packages from her hands.

"Eva and I went shopping," she explained needlessly.

"Daddy, can I sing the song now?" Eric asked.

"In a second, Eric. We came to see if you would take another chance with us."

"But you weren't home," Eric added. "We've been waiting and waiting."

"So you said. I didn't know you were coming or I could have told you I wouldn't be home."

"If I'd called ahead, which I didn't. My fault," Jared said.

"Can I see Cocoa?" Eric asked when they reached her apartment.

Susannah wasn't at all sure about spending any

more time with Jared, but she couldn't refuse Eric's plea.

"Sure. He'll be happy to see you again."

A few moments later Eric blissfully held a lapful of purring kitty. Susannah took the packages to her room and dumped them on the bed. Pausing in front of the mirror before returning to the living room, she stared at her reflection.

Eva had been right. Just styling her hair had made a huge difference. The layered look was perfect. The new makeup enhanced her eyes. She'd put on a few pounds, indulging in hot-fudge sundaes. She looked good!

Susannah entered the living room in time to hear Eric singing softly. She recognized the tune as "Oh Susannah", but he was a bit off the mark saying he knew all the words. He seemed to be able to sing only "Oh" and "Susannah".

"Are we going now?" he asked when he saw her.

"Going already?" she asked, surprised at the disappointment she felt. They'd just arrived.

"You can come, too. We came to 'vite you. Can Cocoa come, too?" Eric asked, not explaining things well.

Susannah looked at Jared in confusion.

"We came to invite you to spend the weekend with us. I have a place about an hour outside of town, near Surrey Junction. We're going up this afternoon to make sure it's ready for winter," Jared interposed.

"We'll stay the night and be back sometime tomorrow afternoon."

Susannah stared at Jared. He was asking her to join them for the weekend. This was beyond helping her. Maybe he did want to see her for herself.

"It's nice," Eric offered hopefully when she didn't respond immediately.

"I'm sure it is."

"Can Cocoa come, too?"

Susannah shook her head. She wasn't even sure she was going. "Cocoa is an apartment cat, he has to stay inside. It's too cold outside for him."

"It's a regular house, not a cabin in the woods. There are three bedrooms. We'd each have our own room. We could go on a hike tomorrow before we return home. You'd be back before dinner. Would that work?" Jared explained.

She felt a mixture of anticipation, excitement and trepidation. Looking at Jared, she tried to ignore the feelings that blossomed whenever he was around. She had to get on with her life, gain independence, not cling to another person.

But she couldn't help wanting to spend more time with Jared. And she liked his son. He was so fortunate to have such a great relationship with his little boy. She envied him that.

So why not go? She had nothing else to do this weekend. It was time she had fun, as Eva was constantly saying.

"Let me pack a few things and I'll be ready."

As she hurried to put some things in her small car-ryall, she marveled at what she was doing. A month ago she'd been in prison with no hope of ever being free. Now she had an apartment, a job and was going off for a weekend with a man and his son.

And she wasn't going to think too much about what this weekend meant.

SOON THEY WERE speeding their way west from the city toward the tree-covered Rockies. Traffic was light. Jared put in a CD that played soft jazz. Eric talked a mile a minute as he questioned Susannah about anything he could think of, asking his father for verification on facts he thought he knew about the house and the deer they sometimes saw from the deck.

"And it snows," he finished dramatically.

"As it does in most of Colorado," Jared said, flick-ing an amused glance at her.

"Do you get to use the house very much?" she asked. It was obvious both Walkers loved the place.

"Not as much as I'd like. I originally bought it with a view to commuting from there to work. It's not that long a drive. But my hours are too erratic and long to make it easy, so I visit when I can on weekends and live out of the apartment during the week."

"There's a fireplace and everything," Eric contrib-uted.

"Sounds wonderful." She looked out of the win-dow, watching the passing scenery, feeling that closed-in feeling starting to take hold. Trying to be unobtrusive, she pressed her hand against the glass, as if absorbing the freedom of the outdoors. It was pathetic she couldn't enjoy everyday things like ordinary people. But the fear began to clutch at her.

"Are you all right?" Jared asked a few moments later.

She glanced at him and nodded, swallowing hard.

"You look pale."

"I, uh— Could we pull off somewhere for a couple of minutes?"

"There's an exit less than a mile ahead, I'll pull off there."

He didn't question her, for which she was grateful. When he pulled to a stop at the edge of the road by the off-ramp, she opened the door and bolted from the car. Taking deep breaths of crisp cold air, Susannah gradually felt herself getting back in control.

Jared joined her by the open field. "What's wrong? Carsick?"

She shook her head. "It's my claustrophobia. Sorry. How much farther is it? Maybe I should just wait here until you two come back tomorrow," she said, trying to make a joke.

"It's still another half hour. But we can take it in stages. Come on, I'll get Eric and we'll walk for a little while."

"You don't have to do that." She felt so foolish. Yet couldn't deny the thought of getting right back into the car was disturbing.

"This is an adventure," Eric said when he joined her, holding tightly to his father's hand. "We've never stopped before."

"Well, I'm sorry we have to stop now," she murmured.

"I'm not. Can I swing?"

"What?"

"He likes it when two adults hold his hands and lift him so he can swing between them. If you think you're up to it, let's give it a try," Jared said.

They walked along the shoulder of the country road, swinging Eric and listening to his laughter. When the car was almost out of sight, Jared suggested they return.

"I'm sorry," Susannah said as they reached the car. "I hope I can hold out until we get there."

"Anytime you need to stop, just let me know," Jared said opening the door. "There's no law that says we have to make the trip nonstop."

Perhaps because he was so understanding, Susannah was able to control the panic attack until they turned on the long, graveled drive to the house. Soaring lodgepole pines covered the hills on either side. In the clearing she saw the large home. Constructed of dark wood, it blended in with the setting as if it had been set down there a hundred years ago. The wide, covered deck in front was obviously used a lot in summer. There were lounge chairs and tables and even a rocking chair.

"It's lovely," she said. As soon as he stopped, she

climbed out of the car, glad to be back in fresh air. If it wasn't so cold, she would have had the window down the entire trip.

"I can see why you want to live here. I'd never leave if it were my place!" She turned around, studying the view from all directions. For the first time in years, she felt at peace. Maybe she should give serious thought to moving out of Denver to the countryside.

Jared and Eric got the bags from the car.

"Come on, Susannah, I'll show you my room in this house," Eric said, tugging on her hand.

"I'll be there in just a minute. Let me see everything out here first," she said, relishing the sense of space.

"Take your time," Jared said. "I'll join you as soon as I get these inside."

Susannah climbed the three steps to the deck and wandered to the far edge. There was a break in the trees and she felt she could see forever. It was quiet and peaceful. How could he stand the hectic pace of Denver knowing he had this haven anytime he wanted?

"Are you okay?" Jared rejoined her on the deck.

She nodded, turning to smile at him. "I'm sorry—"

He raised his hand. "Do not say that again. You can't help feeling that way. How did you deal with it in prison?"

"Not well. The first couple of years, I had to be

medicated or I'd have gone entirely crazy. But Marissa helped me cope. We'd sit with our eyes closed and imagine we were on the beach somewhere, or flying like an eagle, or something." She owed her friend such a debt. She couldn't imagine what she would have done if Marissa hadn't been there.

"It wasn't so bad when the weather was good. I spent a lot of time outside in the gardens. But winters were hard, being inside all the time," she finished.

"I wish I could make it up to you, Susannah," he said in a low voice. "I am so sorry for everything that happened to you."

"You got me out, that's what I'll dwell on from now on. Those eight years can't ever be given back. I can't get my baby back, or Shawn, or my teaching career. But at least I'm out and free. You will never know how wonderful that is."

"No, not in the same sense. But— Never mind."

"What?"

He leaned against the railing, his gaze in the distance. "I married Noelle for several reasons, and by the time we got divorced, I felt as if I had been a prison of my own making. The freedom afterward was heady. I knew then the full extent of what I'd become and done to try to gain something that didn't even mean much in the greater scheme of things."

"I'm confused," Susannah said. "What are you talking about?"

He turned slightly to face her. "I came from the wrong side of the tracks. Got a scholarship to college, majored in pre-law, then went on for the law degree. Your case was my first big criminal case. And I so wanted to prove I could do it to impress Noelle and her family.''

''So they'd accept you?''

''Something like that. Timothy Winters is Noelle's cousin.''

''What?'' Susannah felt as if someone had smacked her. She hadn't known of the relationship. ''Wasn't that a conflict of interest or something, you being on the prosecution's team and involved with a member of the victim's family?''

''We were only casually dating at the time. We got engaged shortly after Christmas that year, married the following summer. No conflict. I didn't contribute much to the proceedings if you'll remember,'' he said.

''So you two married and things weren't perfect?'' Some of her charity for the man waned learning this new tidbit. And she couldn't believe how Noelle had behaved toward her considering it was her cousin who had caused Susannah's situation to begin with. Maybe Noelle thought Susannah knew, and had had a double reason for revenge.

''As a kid I always thought people who lived like the Winters had it made. The reality turned out to be different. I got tired of endless rounds of parties, of Noelle buying new clothes after wearing a dress only once or twice. Of squeezing in time for vacations and weekend jaunts when I wanted to focus on work.''

"Work is so important?" she asked, curious now where this was leading.

"Whether or not you believe me, I became a prosecuting attorney to put away criminals. The system works most of the time. Not in your case, but—" He stopped.

"But what?"

"I started to say the circumstances were unique for you. If it hadn't been an election year, if Michael hadn't been so cocksure of himself, if you'd drawn a different judge, a different public defender, who knows what the outcome would have been."

"You do. You know it was wrong. That's why I'm out, because when you looked at it again, you knew I was innocent."

"I also have eight years of experience now that I lacked then. I can't change the past."

She sighed and shrugged. "No one can. Just lucky me, I got caught up in it, right?"

Eric came to the door. "Are you coming to see my room, Susannah? Then we can go hiking, right, Daddy?"

"No hiking today, kid," Jared said. "It'll be dark soon."

"But you said we're going hiking. I wanted to go to the creek. Susannah hasn't seen it. I wanted to go today!"

"Not now, it's getting too late."

"That's not fair!" Eric pouted and kicked at the

doorjamb. The long drive had obviously taken its toll on the five-year-old.

"Tell you what, you can help with dinner," Jared said as a diversion. It worked.

"Are we having hot dogs on sticks?" Eric asked excitedly.

"Of course." Jared touched her lightly on the shoulder, turning her toward the door. "I hope you like hot dogs grilled over an open fire. It's Eric's favorite winter meal."

"One I bet his mother doesn't indulge in often." Oh, that was catty, she thought, glancing at Jared.

Jared grinned at her, and Susannah felt her heart skip a beat. What would it be like to feel completely at ease around the man? To explore where this shimmering feeling of attraction would lead? Where did she want it to lead?

"Noelle doesn't even eat hot dogs cooked the conventional way, I'm sure she'd be horrified to learn how we cook them. It's Eric's and my secret. Don't give us away," Jared said.

Susannah laughed. She could imagine Noelle Walker looking down her nose at their campfire cooking. A feeling of euphoria replaced her somber mood of earlier. She couldn't change the past, but she could enjoy her present. And for this weekend, her present included Jared and Eric Walker.

BY THE TIME Eric was in bed, Susannah felt comfortable. They had easily managed dinner, despite her fears that Eric would burn his hot dog to a crisp. He liked it slightly charred, he assured her.

Darkness had fallen. The living area was cozy with the fire in the fireplace, quiet now that Eric had gone to sleep.

"Why did you invite me here, Jared?" Susannah asked, gazing at the fire.

"I thought you'd enjoy a break from Denver."

"I just got there a couple of weeks ago."

"You strike me as the outdoors type. You're always going for walks, like to work outside," he said.

"Beats being cooped up inside."

"Tomorrow we'll hike up to a little creek. It spills over rocks and winds down the hillside. Even this late in the year, water is flowing. In the spring when the snow melts you can hear it from almost half a mile away."

"How much land do you have here?" she asked.

"About twelve acres. Five acres around the house and seven acres across the road. Not much good for anything but growing trees and keeping neighbors from being too close."

Feeling restless, she rose and paced to the window, peering out into the night. The walls were starting to close in. She couldn't get any sense of space from the darkness beyond the windows.

"I wouldn't mind taking one of those walks now," she murmured.

"It's pitch-dark outside."

"Maybe I'll just step out onto the deck."

"And cold."

"Then the fire will feel doubly warm when I return." She took her jacket off the coatrack and went out onto the deck. The lights from the windows gleamed and gave her enough illumination. She walked over and leaned against the railing. It was cold, but quiet and peaceful. Would she and Shawn ever have been able to afford a place like this?

She'd moved so much as a kid she'd longed to put down roots and never move again. Shawn had liked Boulder growing up, he'd said, but wanted more excitement and opportunity. Once he had moved up in his career as an engineer, would he have been content to move away from the big city?

Maybe everything would have been different that summer if she'd known she was pregnant.

"I hope you are all right, baby girl," she whispered softly. She missed her child every day. The anguish had grown stronger since she'd been released. She'd known all along, of course, that she was innocent. Giving up her baby had been difficult, but without a hope of parole, it hadn't been fair to tie a young child up in the legal system.

But now. If only she'd put her in foster care, she could claim her child. They could make a life together, laughing, cooking hot dogs over an open flame, singing songs. Being with Eric brought home more than anything all she'd missed, and would forever miss, with her own daughter.

Tears filled her eyes. She blinked, but they spilled

over. Life had been unfair. She had to deal with it and move on. But it was so hard.

"You've been out here a long time. Come back inside," Jared said. He stood beside her. She hadn't heard him come out.

"In a minute," she said.

He turned her until her face was in the lamplight from the window.

"Don't cry, Susannah. I'm so sorry." He wrapped her in his arms and hugged her tightly against him.

Before she could struggle to be free his mouth found hers and he kissed her.

She had not been touched in years. She was filled with anger and hurt and bitterness. But the touch of his mouth on hers gave her a surge of feminine delight. The shock of the unexpected kiss gave her a pulse of life she hadn't felt before. His hands didn't hurt, they caressed. His body didn't threaten, it provided strength she could cling to. His mouth didn't denigrate, but cherished.

Then reality returned. He was kissing her as a man kisses a woman. Not as a favor, not as atonement. His mouth moved persuasively against hers, coaxing a response she became willing to give. When he parted her lips and his tongue danced with hers, she felt more alive since the nightmare of her life had begun eight years ago.

Gently he took her on an exploration of senses she never wanted to end. The blood pounded through her as she forgot old fears and dangers and was swept away. Moments melted into moments. Time was suspended, or raced, she wasn't sure which.

Slowly he gentled the kiss, then pulled back.

She shivered when he lifted his head from hers, afraid to see what might be in his eyes.

"It's cold, let's go inside," he suggested, his hands on her shoulders, his head bent slightly to see her.

"If you're cold after that kiss, we weren't on the same wavelength," she said, trying to lighten the moment. She wasn't at all sure how to act.

"I'd like to think we were on the same wavelength. But it's getting windy."

She took a deep breath of the cold air and nodded, slipping from beneath his hands. "I'm ready to go in." She walked the short distance to the front door, scrambling around in her mind for something to talk about. Once in the lighted room, there'd be no hiding from their kiss.

JARED HELD the door for her and followed her inside. He couldn't believe he'd kissed her. And that she'd responded. He wanted her, as he hadn't wanted another woman in a long time. But he was not going to blunder into anything. He had to take things slowly. He was lucky she hadn't hauled off and slugged him. Would she ever see beyond the trial eight years ago, to see him as a man who might be interested in forging some kind of relationship?

"Do you want some more hot chocolate? Or something else?" He was feeling as tongue-tied as a teenager with a crush on a cheerleader. He wanted her to relax, but from the way she hugged herself and stood so rigid near the fireplace, he'd made her more uncomfortable.

"Hot chocolate sounds great," she said politely.

"Coming up." He went to the kitchen, kicking himself for making her nervous. They had the rest of the evening to get through, and all day tomorrow. He had hoped the break would be fun. Now she was probably thinking—

"Can I help?" Susannah asked from the doorway.

"Want marshmallows?"

"Of course, what's hot chocolate without them?"

"They're in the cupboard there," he gestured, "if you want to get them."

Maybe he hadn't blown things. While she hadn't warmed up as much as he might wish, she didn't seem any more wary than normal.

"So, tell me, what are we doing tomorrow? I don't have hiking boots, you know," she said, sitting on one of the high stools by the breakfast nook.

"We'll have breakfast, then go for a walk. Nothing strenuous—Eric can't go far. But I think you'll like it. He loves going to the creek. We'll try to skip rocks, or have a throwing contest. We'll come back for lunch and then head for town."

"If I had this place, I'd stay here all the time," she said. "Any skiing nearby?"

"Just cross-country through the trees. Do you ski?" he asked.

"Shawn took me a couple of times when we were in college. I didn't progress fast, I was still on the bunny slopes." She smiled sadly, and Jared knew she was lost in the past again.

"Where did you grow up?"

"I was a military brat. My father was in the army. We moved a lot."

"He's dead, right?" Jared asked. He remembered how alone she'd been during the trial.

"He died while I was in college, in a skirmish overseas. After my mother died when I was five, it was just my father and me, But he was often too busy with his career to notice me."

"Grandparents?"

She shook her head.

"I was an only child, my father was an orphan, and my mother was a menopause baby, so her parents were quite a bit older. They both died shortly after she did."

So her daughter was literally her only family in the world. And thanks to Michael Denning and him, she had no contact with her child. Jared vowed he'd find her for Susannah. If only to give her peace of mind.

When the chocolate was ready, they moved back into the living room. Susannah sat on one of the chairs. To keep a safe distance, he thought wryly. He didn't blame her.

"So tell me how you found this place and what you do here year-round. Skiing in winter, hiking in fall. What about summer?" she asked.

Jared told her about how they waded in the creek after the snow melted in the spring, freezing their feet and ankles. By late summer it was shallow enough to warm up by midday in the sun. Then they could swim and play in the deeper pools. Eric loved it. He told her how Eric liked seeing deer from the deck, or the squirrels that chattered so constantly during the warm weather.

She listened and laughed. He was struck by how different she looked from the woman he'd taken to dinner that first night. Her hair was shining and feathered around her head. Her eyes sparkled and her cheeks had a rosy glow from the cold.

He was fascinated by her, wanted to learn more about what she planned to do with her future. Hear her views on raising children, or planting a garden. Enjoy her laughter for more than one evening.

"It's getting late. I think I'll go to bed," she said, rising. She carried her empty cup into the kitchen.

He heard the water run. Glancing at his watch, he counted the hours until they'd be up again.

"DADDY MAKES the bestest pancakes," Eric said the next morning when he and Susannah were settled at the breakfast nook, seated on the high stools. Jared felt a glow at his son's praise. How long before reality took hold and Eric realized his father was a mere mortal, one who made mistakes like everyone else?

Too soon, he feared. But for the time being, he liked his son's adoration.

"I can't wait to eat the world's bestest pancakes," Susannah responded. "Do you like lots of syrup on them?"

"Yes, and sometimes jelly. I like strawberry—what do you like?"

"Grape is my favorite."

It was a terrible thing when a man was jealous of his five-year-old son, but Jared was feeling left out. Susannah never asked his preferences, never asked about his life or his past. Was he fooling himself in thinking something might develop between them? Was she going along just until they found Timothy? Or was she justifiably wary and untrusting?

Maybe the attraction wasn't two-sided.

He liked that idea least of all.

SUSANNAH TRIED not to watch Jared. She was conscious of his son sitting beside her. Who knew what a little boy would observe and then tell his mother?

But her gaze drifted that way time and time again. She couldn't believe he had kissed her last night. Or that he'd even invited her away for the weekend for that matter. Was it further atonement for his part in what had happened? Or was he seriously interested in her?

Did she want him to be?

It was too early to be thinking of any kind of relationship. She had her life to get back on track. And there could be no closure for her until Timothy Winters had been caught.

Eric was an enthusiastic tour guide when they started on their walk. He pointed out places he and his father played at in the summer.

The temperature was below freezing. Despite the sunshine, they needed to keep moving to stay warm. It felt glorious to tramp through the trees, free and unencumbered. There was nothing on her mind but the moment. Susannah was grateful she had come.

Lunch was quickly over and they were on the road back to Denver before Susannah was ready for the weekend to end.

"Can we go up and see the cat?" Eric asked when they reached Susannah's apartment.

Jared looked at her. She nodded, glad to postpone farewells for a little longer. "Cocoa is probably lonely after being alone since yesterday, I'll bet he'll be glad to see us," she said. "Do you have time?"

"We have plenty of time. Eric doesn't go home until after dinner."

Was that a hint he wasn't any more anxious to have the day end than she?

CHAPTER TEN

JARED GREETED his secretary when he entered the office Tuesday morning, pausing at her frantic gesture.

"Something wrong?"

"I'd say. There's a processor server in your office," she whispered.

Curious, Jared walked in his office and greeted the uniformed deputy. He took the papers the man offered and waited until he left before opening them. Noelle was suing to change the custody agreement—requesting restriction of visitation to supervised visits only, citing him as a dangerous influence on their son. Until the court ruled on the decision, he was ordered to stay away from Eric.

He stared at the papers. What was she thinking? How could she have managed that so quickly? Of course, with her family connections, anything was possible. Judge Perle was a friend of her parents, and she'd probably appealed to him yesterday morning once she'd learned from Eric that Susannah had accompanied them on their weekend away. He had not told his son to keep quiet about their guest. There was no need for secrecy, nothing had happened.

He thought about the kiss, then dismissed it. There

had been nothing wrong with it. In fact, the kiss had been more along the lines of mind-blowing.

Jared's anger at Noelle simmered. Eric was his son, too, and he was entitled to raise him as he saw fit.

If Noelle wanted to play hardball, she'd come to the right place. He reached for the phone and called the attorney who had handled his divorce.

When the call concluded, he dialed Noelle.

"I know why you're calling, and I don't want to talk to you," she said.

"I'm calling to say I've petitioned to have the injunction suspended. And I've filed for joint custody."

"What? You can't do that!"

"I can and have. Once my attorney presents the facts to a family law judge later this week, your injunction will be rescinded. But I'm serious about petitioning for joint custody. Weekends aren't enough anymore."

"You're a bad influence on him."

"Give it up, Noelle. I'm not a bad influence and if you try to use Susannah, that'll blow up in your face, too. How many times do I have to tell you she did not kill anyone. She was innocent and the record has been expunged."

"Let's discuss this rationally," she said. "And not on the phone. Take me to dinner tonight."

"I'm busy," he said. He was not going to jump through hoops for Noelle.

"Seeing your little jailbird again?" she asked with an edge to her tone.

"I'm not going to discuss that with you now or at any other time."

"Then I'll see you in court. And we'll just see what a judge says. I'm much better equipped to take care of our son than you are. Your long hours will work against you in this, Jared. What would you do with joint custody? Place him in child-care for hours each day? Compare that to the home life he now enjoys. How do you think a judge will rule?"

She hung up before he could respond.

He took a careful breath and replaced the receiver. She had a point. But millions of other children spent after-school hours in day care and didn't suffer because of it. It would only be a few hours a day. Jared would take his son to school, pick him up after work and spend evenings with him.

Noelle did have a definite advantage, however. Even more so since she'd gotten Judge Perle to issue the injunction. While judges were supposed to be impartial, he knew there was a lot of back-room negotiations and favors called. The Winters family had always been generous with campaign funds and other support for the local judiciary.

He'd have to make sure his attorney drew a totally impartial judge with no ties to the Winters family. It was time he played a bigger part in Eric's life.

"CALL FOR YOU," Pete yelled across the planting floor to Susannah on Friday afternoon. He held up the phone.

"Who would call me?" she murmured, dusting the dirt from her hand.

"I hope it's not reporters who found out where you work," Eva said next to her. "If so, just say no comment and hang up."

"Hello?" she said when Pete handed her the phone.

"Susannah, Jared here. The police in San Francisco just called. They believe they'll have Timothy in custody within the hour. I'm flying out to San Francisco tonight. Do you want to come with me?"

Her heart pounded. Timothy caught! He would have the answers. He could make some sense of this whole thing.

"Yes, yes, I do. When would we leave?"

"I'm having Rose look into tickets now. Probably the first flight out this evening. We'll plan to be back Sunday night so you won't miss work. I'll call you when you get home to tell you what time I'll pick you up."

"Okay. I'll be home by six."

She walked back to her worktable in a daze. Timothy would be in custody before long. Everyone who'd ever doubted her would know the truth—she had never killed anyone. What would she do when she saw him? What would he say, what could he say, to make sense of the past eight years?

"Bad news?" Eva asked.

"Good news, I think. The cops in San Francisco believe they'll have Timothy in custody tonight. Jared asked me to fly there with him. I'm going to get to talk to Timothy after all. I never thought Jared would let me see him.''

Eva glanced at Susannah, then asked, ''What will you say to Timothy?''

''Mostly I want answers. How could he have killed someone and then made it look like I did it? Why? He must hate me.''

''Or he was just looking out for his own skin.''

SUSANNAH WAS ON tenterhooks by the time Jared picked her up at seven. They had a ten o'clock flight direct to San Francisco.

It hadn't taken her long to pack. She hadn't eaten, fretting about the departure time. She hoped she could choke down something on the plane, but she wasn't sure she could keep anything in her churning stomach.

''Have you heard anything new?'' she asked Jared after greeting him at the door.

''Nothing more. I'll check in with SFPD when we land. That's all you have?'' he asked.

She nodded. ''I feel funny leaving Cocoa again this weekend. He's going to think I'm only a part-time cat-watcher,'' she said as they went to the car.

''He'll appreciate you even more during the week.''

''How's Eric? Was he upset you aren't spending the weekend with him?'' she asked once they were in the vehicle and speeding toward the airport.

"Disappointed, I think, but this is not the first time I've had business interfere with our plans. He understands."

"As long as he's not disappointed too often," she murmured, wondering if the little boy did understand.

"What do you mean?" Jared asked.

"That was my father's excuse—the army always came first. Truth to tell, I think he either didn't like me much, or had no idea what to do with a child."

Jared looked at her. "Then he shouldn't have had children."

"I don't know. When he and my mother were married, they thought they had the entire world ahead of them. It wasn't his fault that five years after I came along she died. If she had lived, things might have been quite different. It takes two to bring a child into the world, and I think we're supposed to have two parents to raise us. It doesn't always work out that way, but I think that's the original plan."

"Life interferes sometimes."

"I know, but we do the best we can."

"I'll miss Eric this weekend, but this is important, too," Jared said.

"I appreciate your taking me. I probably wouldn't stand a chance to see him once he's been extradited to Colorado, would I?"

"Not before the trial. Afterward, I think he'd get to say if he wanted to see you or not."

"Thank you, Jared."

THE JOURNEY was uneventful. Susannah sat by the window, staring out at the stars, ignoring her sense of disquiet. She would not get claustrophobia on the airplane. There was no going for a walk at thirty-thousand feet.

She sipped a cola hoping to settle the butterflies. She nibbled on peanuts and stared out the window into the darkness, watching the blinking lights on the wing. What would she say to Timothy? What could he say to make everything all right—nothing. Still, she had to see him.

No matter what the outcome, she was grateful Jared had included her. According to Eva, that wasn't the norm at all, and might even get him in hot water.

She glanced at Jared. He was working on some papers he'd brought in his briefcase. He was a confident man. She suspected he wasn't a bit worried about the outcome.

She wished she had some of his self-assurance.

After a full day of work, and the emotional toll of learning Timothy was about to be captured, plus the flight from Denver, Susannah was dead tired when they reached San Francisco.

She had never been to California before, but the freeway looked much like the ones in Denver in the dark, and there was little to see.

Jared had reserved rooms at a hotel near the Civic Center, and before long she was behind her door, about to fall asleep standing. Yet once in bed, she was too keyed up to sleep.

Scenes from that last summer, from the trial and

from her years in prison flooded her memory. She tried deep breathing. Tossed and turned. Nothing worked. She was tired, but not sleepy.

On a whim, she lifted the phone and asked the front desk for Jared's room.

"Walker."

His voice was strong coming through the line in the darkness of her room.

"Hi, it's Susannah. Did I wake you? I couldn't sleep."

"No, I was reviewing some of the files. I checked with the police, Timothy is resting in one of their cells as we speak. We won't have much of a chance to catch Timothy unaware, or without an attorney for long. I want to elicit certain facts as quickly as possible." He paused. Then said, "Justice can prevail, however delayed."

"That's why you do this, isn't it? For justice," she said thoughtfully.

He was quiet a long moment. "I know life is unfair, bad things happen to good people. But if I can balance the scales a bit, then it makes what I do worthwhile."

"I imagine Noelle is furious over the turn of events," she said, remembering the scene at Jared's apartment. "He is her cousin."

"She's more upset over us," he replied.

Susannah felt a shiver of excitement. "Us?"

"She thinks…"

"What?"

"That there's something between us."

It was Susannah's turn to fall quiet. She wondered if the feelings she had for Jared were something to build on, or if they were just gratitude. She wondered if there was any possible future for her with any man.

There was so much baggage, from her father, from Shawn's death, from losing her baby and the distrust she had of everything.

Could she ever have faith in a relationship again? In another person?

"You still there?" he asked.

"Yes."

"Don't worry about what Noelle thinks. In the greater scheme of things, it's only important to Noelle."

"Do you think she's right?" she asked, almost holding her breath as she waited for his answer.

"How do you feel about it?"

She gave the question some thought. "I enjoy being with you," she said at last. It conveyed her immediate feelings, but left the future open.

"I enjoy being with you," he replied.

"Maybe we should leave it there for the time being," she said.

"Or explore where it could lead us," he countered.

"I thought you were burned out on relationships after your marriage."

"I'm not saying we need to rush into a lifelong

relationship. I enjoy your company. I think we can muddle through this weekend together, don't you?"

"I suppose."

He was hedging. And how clear did she need it— *not a lifelong relationship.* Still, a glimmer of hope came unbidden. She was tired of being alone. Fearful of a lonely future of going through the motions of living. She'd loved Shawn with all the passion of her youth. Had he lived, she was sure they would have had a happy life together. But he was gone.

She was a different person. Could she take that next step?

Not yet, but maybe one day. And if not with Jared, then with someone she could trust and fall in love with.

"Maybe," she said, afraid she was wishing too much for something that couldn't be.

She needed to make sure what she felt was more than gratitude.

"Order warm milk from room service and try to get some sleep," he said. "I'll call you around eight. We'll have breakfast and then check in with the police. Sleep well."

"Good night," she said slowly and waited to hear him hang up before replacing the receiver.

His suggestion hadn't been the sleep inducer she needed. Now her thoughts were jumbled remembering every time she'd seen or spoke with Jared, from those awful days at the trial, through his initial visit at the prison to their dinner that first night out.

But it was the more recent events that dominated—the fun day at the zoo with Eric, visiting his home in the mountains. The kiss on the deck.

Thinking on that kiss, Susannah finally drifted to sleep.

JARED ROSE AND PACED. Her phone call had been unexpected. And he was surprised he'd opened up as much as he had. Usually he kept his feelings close. But he was tired of the status quo. He wanted more. Despite his words to the contrary, maybe it was time he looked for a long-lasting relationship. He had enjoyed being part of a couple. Liked the idea of someone at home waiting for him each night, who would share his high points and lows. And someone he could be himself with.

He went to the window and looked out over the sparkling skyline of San Francisco. Idly he wondered why so many lights were on in the high-rise buildings. Were men and women working late, trying to make it to the top?

Cleaning staff, most likely. It was after midnight. But then, he'd spent nights at the office working until long past that. For what?

He had always taken pride in his place in the judicial system. Now he questioned his beliefs. He was appalled at how such a miscarriage of justice could have occurred. He wanted to sweep Susannah off her feet and shower her with all the things she'd missed.

Take her to dinner, dancing. To a few plays, or the symphony. Maybe try skiing or skating.

But the only thing he could truly bring that she couldn't get anywhere else would be news of her daughter.

He'd been quietly working his way through clerks, recorders and other minions of the courthouse. With any luck, he'd find the answers he was looking for.

Once he was sure her daughter was well and happy, he could reassure Susannah.

He knew the risk. She could insist on petitioning the courts to reverse the adoption, citing the wrongful conviction as the only reason she gave up her child.

He thought of Eric, and tried again to imagine how it would feel to give him up completely.

"Timothy Winters, you have a lot to answer for," he said, gazing out into the night.

SUSANNAH WAS READY the next morning when Jared called. They met at the elevator and rode down to the lobby. Soon seated at the coffee shop that served the hotel, they ordered, then fell silent.

Susannah looked around her, not knowing what to say. The usual amenities had already been dealt with: how did you sleep, how are you today? Their conversation from last night lingered in her mind. Should she say something about that or ignore it in the light of day?

"How long before we can go see Timothy?"

"I called the detective this morning, we can see him as soon as we finish eating."

"Let's go now," Susannah said. She couldn't eat a thing anyway. The wait was over. She wanted to see him immediately.

"Not until we have breakfast. They're expecting us around nine-thirty, so we have plenty of time."

"I'm not hungry."

"I am," he said mildly.

Then he surprised her by reaching out to take her hand in his, squeezing it gently. "I know you've waited a long time for this, but he's not going anywhere. You didn't have dinner last night. You need to eat."

She took a breath to blast him with some pithy comment, then exhaled slowly. He was right. Timothy was caught at last. She could eat before she confronted him.

"I'll have toast."

"Well, I'm having the full spread—eggs, bacon, hash browns and muffin. You might as well eat as much since you'll still have to wait for me to finish."

"Did anyone ever tell you that you're manipulative and bossy?" she asked, trying to stifle her frustration.

He gave her a slow smile that about melted her heart. "I've heard it said."

"Well, you are," she grumbled, looking away before she did something foolish. It was only a smile. So why did her heart rate increase?

"What are you planning to say to him?" Jared asked, releasing her hand.

She wished he hadn't let go. Surprised at her reaction, she looked at him. Was she finally getting over her fears? Or was it just with Jared?

"I'm not sure. I guess I can't slug him a couple of times?" she asked.

"Not allowed, though I'd be first in line after you if it were."

"Then I'll ask him why he set me up. I know he didn't like me as much as he liked Shawn, but to condemn someone to life in prison for nothing, I don't get it."

"I hope you get the answers you want," he said.

When their meals were served, Jared asked her if she wanted to see some of San Francisco after they finished with Timothy.

"I don't know. I hadn't thought beyond seeing him." She looked around as if awakening from a deep sleep. "It's the first time I've been here, so I guess I should make the most of it. Who knows if or when I'll come again. Have you been here before?"

"A couple of times. It's a beautiful city. We'll see the highlights, have a relaxed weekend and head for home tomorrow."

"If we finish early, we could be back in Denver tonight. You could still see Eric for part of the weekend."

"Eric's not expecting me, so we could stay."

"Then I want to ride a cable car," Susannah said firmly.

He nodded. "And visit Fisherman's Wharf, eat in Chinatown, and walk where we will. It's a great city for walking despite the hills."

"But first, Timothy."

"First Timothy Winters."

CHAPTER ELEVEN

PROMPTLY AT NINE-THIRTY, Jared and Susannah arrived at the police station. Detective Benson greeted them, verified Jared's identification and took them back to an interrogation room. Susannah was introduced simply as Jared's assistant. She realized the police officer might recognize her name if he'd learned much about the situation.

"We've got Winters, or John Wiley as he insists is his name, in one of the interview rooms. He had identification for Wiley. We've run background checks and can't find information on the man prior to about seven years ago. No school records, no family, the works."

He paused by a door. "Want me in with you?" he asked Jared.

Jared nodded. "He ask for an attorney yet?"

"No, claims we have the wrong man. Seems cool and collected. You give us the word and we'll book him for murder one."

"With extradition to Colorado."

"That paperwork is in process. He's all yours if he's the right man." Detective Benson opened the door and stepped inside. "I've brought someone you might know," he said.

Jared followed him in and looked at Timothy. He hadn't known Noelle's cousin well, but had met him on occasion. The eight years since he'd last seen him had been good ones for Timothy. He looked hale and hearty. And puzzled. It was a nice touch.

"I don't believe we've met," he said.

"You may not remember me, I was dating your cousin Noelle last time I saw you," Jared said, placing his briefcase on the table.

"I have no cousins," Timothy said.

"Hello, Timothy, maybe you'll remember me, even if you don't remember your cousin Noelle," Susannah said, moving from behind Jared.

Timothy paled when he saw her. His poise fled and he looked wildly around the room as if seeking an escape route.

"I want a lawyer," he told Detective Benson.

"That can be arranged," the detective said lazily. "But first these folks have come all the way from Denver to see you. Don't you want to talk to them?"

"No. Get me an attorney."

"Who was the man you killed?" Jared asked.

"I didn't kill anyone. She did," he pointed to Susannah. "I thought you'd gone to prison. What are you doing out?"

"So you knew. I had hoped all along you'd run out, never knowing I'd been charged and convicted," she said. This man had been Shawn's friend—how could he have let her go to prison?

"What's this?" Detective Benson asked, startled by their conversation. He turned to Susannah. "Who are you?"

"It's okay, I'll explain later," Jared murmured. He leaned against the wall and crossed his arms, looking at Timothy.

"You killed the man who lived with you. Pinned the rap on Susannah and disappeared. Everyone thought you'd been the one killed. Once we realized you weren't dead, all motive for her doing the crime vanished. She's been out of prison for several weeks now, no thanks to you," Jared said.

"She killed Todd. Since Shawn, the love of her life, was gone, she wanted payback. So she killed the man I loved," he said desperately. "She's your killer, not me."

"I didn't even know Todd," she said approaching the table. "Did you know Shawn and I had a baby? That child was taken from me because I was in prison serving a life sentence. Shawn's dead because of you, Shawn's daughter is living with strangers because of you. For that alone, I hope they lock you up forever. How could you do that to me? I thought we were friends."

"I'm not going to prison. I demand an attorney," he shouted, rising. The uniformed police officer standing beside him pressed him back in his chair without a word.

"The courts will decide what happens to you," Jared said. "I don't imagine you'll win any extra points for letting Susannah take the rap for a crime you committed."

"She's a nobody. The Winters family is somebody in Denver."

"No one is above the law."

"Hell, Shawn was dead. What did it matter?" Timothy said grudgingly. "I missed Shawn. It wasn't my fault he died. He shouldn't have let me drive if I'd had too much to drink. He was my friend. What kind of friend lets someone drive when they're drunk?"

Susannah looked at him in growing anger. "You are responsible for your own actions. Grow up. Don't blame Shawn for your own failings. You insisted on driving, Harry testified to that. You killed him. Then you killed that other man. You may be from a fine family, but something got twisted in you."

"Bitch! You took Shawn away from me," Timothy shouted. "He and I planned on doing things together once he was out of college. Only you got your claws into him and changed him."

"What?" Susannah blinked. What was he talking about? "Shawn was your friend, we both were. We were going to settle in Denver because Shawn wanted to live close to you."

Timothy glared at her. "Things changed. He began to want to do more with other couples—straight couples. He told me that night. It was getting awkward for him and you to be doing things with just me. And

I couldn't bring Todd. How long do you think it would have been before my father found out? He'd have cut me off without a dime. If you hadn't taken Shawn, none of this would have happened. You deserved to go to jail.''

''Seems to me disappearing like you did cut you off pretty effectively,'' Jared said.

''By then it was a matter of necessity. I still had a few assets I was able to take with me,'' Timothy muttered, glaring at Susannah.

''That explains why you let Susannah take the rap, but not why you killed Todd in the first place,'' Jared said.

''I didn't kill anyone. I want a lawyer. I have nothing more to say until I see one,'' he said.

''We've got opportunity, means and a connection with the victim. A little digging in the right direction will give us motive, then you're going down for murder one. We might cut a deal if you talk,'' Jared said.

Susannah glared at him. ''Don't you dare cut him some deal. He goes to trial and I hope he gets the maximum they can dish out.''

''It'll never happen, babe,'' Timothy said, rocking back in his chair, that confident look returning. ''I'm a Winters, that name carries a lot of weight in Denver. No one can prove a thing. I'll be out in a couple of days on bail.''

''No bail. You're a flight risk,'' Jared said.

Again Timothy's demeanor faltered, but he recovered. ''No more until I see an attorney.''

"Who was Todd? Last name?" Jared asked.

"I want an attorney," Timothy said.

Jared asked several more questions, but Timothy didn't say another word except to demand legal counsel.

"And that's it," Susannah said when they were leaving the police department. "I was a toss-away because in his mind I stole his friend. All that summer I thought Timothy liked me."

"Sounds to me like the man is demented. But I'm not going to let that be a plea," Jared said.

She stopped at the doorway and looked at him. "Please promise me you'll make sure he gets convicted."

"I'll do my best."

"No, I want a promise."

He looked into her eyes for a long moment. "All right, Susannah, I promise."

OUTSIDE, the air was cool, the sun shining. San Francisco was much more temperate in late November than Denver. She looked around, the beautiful day seemed at odds with the darkness her life had been.

"I still can't believe it. Eight years of my life wasted, and not a drop of remorse in the man. How does someone get to be so unfeeling?"

Jared reached for her arm, swung her gently around until she stood in front of him. "Let it go, Susannah. If you don't, it'll eat you up until you become so embittered you can't enjoy the life you have. He was wrong. We were wrong. It's taken a long time, but it's all turning out right. Justice will be served. You are a young, vibrant woman who had a setback that would have killed many people. Stay strong.''

"Easy for you to say, you didn't lose eight years of your life because someone thought you were expendable. You didn't give up your baby.''

"I'll find your baby,'' he said.

"What?'' Had she heard him correctly? Her heart skipped a beat, then began pounding in her chest. Would he really? Could he?

"I'll find your daughter and let you know if she's all right,'' he said solemnly.

"Can you do that?'' she whispered, afraid to hope, yet yearning so dearly to know her baby was happy, was being raised in a loving family. If only she could see her, touch her, just once, to assure herself.

"Technically, no. But hang regulations. If I can locate her, I'll make sure she's fine and tell you.''

"And if she isn't?'' she asked, fearful he'd wash his hands of her if she pushed, but she had to know.

"Then we'll take steps to remedy the situation.''

"Oh.'' She was going to get reassurance her baby was all right. It was what she wanted. Mostly.

What she truly wanted was to have her child to raise. But that would never happen. And she wouldn't disrupt her daughter's life by claiming her at this point. If she was in a loving home, she wouldn't need Susannah.

The ache was painful as she tried to hold on to the

hope Jared had offered. Reassurance that her daughter was loved and cared for was more than she'd ever expected to know, and it would have to be enough.

"As soon as I know something, I'll tell you. But that won't be today. We're booked on a flight to-morrow afternoon, so let's make the most of the time we have here," he said, slipping his hand down her arm to take her hand in his. "Let's go find the cable cars."

THE REMAINDER of the day was forever imprinted on Susannah's mind as one of endless delight. Jared did his best to help her put Timothy out of her mind.

Once they'd changed into casual clothes, the first thing they did was find the cable cars. She loved hanging onto the vertical poles and standing on the platform, pressing in close to Jared when they passed automobiles or went around corners, leaning back to enjoy the freedom as the gripman rang the bell. The view of San Francisco Bay from the top of Hyde Street was spectacular. The water was a deep blue, dotted with scores of white sails.

Prowling around San Francisco City Center, Susannah was shocked. Prices were even higher than in Denver, and she'd been surprised at how expensive everything was there. She studied the fashions, wandered in the bookstore and bought several books. As soon as she returned to Denver, she'd see about getting a library card. She'd read a lot in prison to pass the evenings hours. Books had provided her only means of escape.

They ate lunch in Chinatown. Then wandered around Little Italy before heading to the wharf.

Pier 39 was glitzy and dazzling, with shops offering everything from sports clothes to Victoriana to old photos of vintage movies. But the chocolate shop was her favorite. She browsed the aisles fascinated by the endless variety. Finally settling on dark chocolate and a box of truffles, she made her purchases and joined Jared waiting patiently by the door.

"You didn't want any?" she asked.

He raised a smaller bag than hers. "I bought Eric a small bag of chocolate coins. I think he'll like them."

Then they wandered around until it was almost dark and the wind from the water was definitely chillier than earlier.

"Want to eat an early dinner and head back to the hotel?" Jared asked.

"Fine." She took a deep breath of the salt-scented air and felt the warm glow of happiness. She almost didn't recognize it for what it was.

"I thought we'd eat at one of the places at Fisherman's Wharf, the seafood is fresh daily."

"That's fine by me," she said, shifting her bag. Jared still carried the books she'd bought, but they had to be getting heavy. "Want me to carry the bags for a while?"

"No." He laced the fingers of his free hand

through hers and pulled her closer as they wandered from Pier 39 toward the older part of Fisherman's Wharf. Lights glittered from the different restaurants that lined the piers.

They chose one and stepped inside. Saturday night was a popular night and even though they were early, the restaurant already had a crowd waiting to be seated.

Susannah pressed against Jared and tried to ignore the other people jammed into the waiting space. Didn't they need more room around them?

Try to think of something else, she admonished herself, shifting her gaze to the room beyond. There was a floor-to-ceiling wall of glass at the far end, giving the appearance the bay was part of the room. She hoped they got a table near the window.

Panic began to nip at her. She shifted around just as she was jostled by someone behind her.

"Careful," Jared said, putting his arm around her shoulders and shifting a bit to gain them some space. "Are you all right? We can try another place."

"Let's," she said, grateful for the offer. She was getting too uncomfortable to enjoy herself. She hated feeling so closed in and there was nothing she could do about it.

Once outside, she drew in another breath of clean air. "Sorry about that," she said. "You can't take me anywhere!"

"Not true. You did fine at the Chinese restaurant

at lunch. Down the street about half a block is an outside café. We'll eat there.''

"It's getting cold," she said, looking at the tables and chairs scattered on the sidewalk.

"They have a heater—see the tall silver thing with the light on top. We'll try it, if it's too uncomfortable we'll think of something else."

Seated moments later, Susannah realized it was perfect. There was no one close by. The radiant heater gave enough warmth that they were comfortable. She enjoyed being able to people watch as other tourists wandered by.

"Perfect," she said, smiling at Jared. "Thank you for a terrific day. I'll always remember it."

"I'm glad you enjoyed it. I did, too."

Jared was surprised at how much he had enjoyed the day. They hadn't done much, hadn't tried to impress anyone, hadn't tried to show off or one-up anyone, which had been his normal experience with Noelle. Today had been about two people enjoying and sharing new experiences together.

In fact, when he thought about it, the day would not have held the same appeal had Susannah not been with him.

He looked at her. Her happiness was obvious.

Since he carried guilt for being a part of taking happiness away from her, he was gratified he'd been able to bring some of it back today. He wished he could insure she'd be happy the rest of her life.

She turned and caught his eye. "What are you having?'' she asked, looking at the menu. "I want one of everything, but don't think I could eat it all.''

"Try anything fresh today.''

"I'll have the mahimahi. My father was stationed in San Diego when I was about ten, and I remember how much I liked it. It's also called dolphin fish and I remember when my dad first told me that, I didn't want to eat it. I thought I'd be eating dolphins.''

"I'm sure the dolphins of the world are relieved.''

She laughed. Then looked at him.

"You know,'' she said slowly, "I don't know very much about you. You always let me do the talking. I'd think an attorney would want to talk more.''

"You don't think I do enough during the course of business?''

"Maybe. Is that why you don't talk around me? Or are you naturally reticent? Tell me about when you were a boy.''

"There's not much to tell. I grew up in Denver. Went to the university, became an attorney and then went to work for the district attorney's office.''

"That's succinct. Who were your friends? Are you still friends today? What did you want to be when you were little? Don't tell me a lawyer, because I'd say more likely a cowboy or fireman.''

"Yeah, I did want to be a cowboy. There were a few kids in my classes who lived on ranches right on the fringes of the school district. To hear them talk was to dream dreams about riding horses, punching cows and winning big in rodeos.''

"Did you ever?"

"No." He hadn't been able to visit them when invited, his dad refused to drive him out. He'd almost forgotten how much he'd wanted to go to Travis Haversham's ranch and learn to ride. Travis had always said they needed help at roundup and if Jared learned to ride, he could join them.

"Just think, if you'd tried that, you might have ended up a rancher rather than a prosecutor."

"I like my job. I hope it's making a difference."

She became quiet and Jared could have kicked himself. Of course it made a difference in her life.

"I'm glad you have your job, too. I don't know if I would have ever been released if someone like you hadn't gone to bat for me."

"Most of the men and women involved are more concerned with justice than glory."

"Most, not all." She shook her head, trying a smile again. "Let's not talk about the past. Let's take a cable car back to the hotel."

"They don't run that far, but we can take one to the end of the line and get a cab from there if you like."

"I would."

MORE PEOPLE were heading toward the wharf than were leaving it by the time Jared and Susannah left. The cable car they hopped on was practically deserted as it moved away from the popular tourist spot.

They sat in silence on the outside bench. Jared held

her hand, tracing his thumb over the back, enjoying the softness of her skin. Was she this soft all over, he wondered. Would he ever find out?

Shifting slightly, he tried to think of something else, but his mind wouldn't give up. He wanted to kiss her. Hold her. Make love to her all night long.

And she probably couldn't wait to get back to her room—alone—take a quick shower and go to bed. Also alone.

There was attraction, and he knew it wasn't all one-sided. But was there anything more? And dare he act on that attraction? Was it too early? Was it skewed by his guilt?

Dammit, he felt as awkward as a teenager on a first date. But it had been a long time since what he did mattered so much. He didn't want to mess up what they did have trying for something more if she wasn't ready.

When they reached their hotel, he carried their bags inside. To the left of the large lobby doors was a bar, soft music was emanating from it.

Susannah looked over and he followed her line of sight. In the back of the bar was a dance floor with several couples moving in time with the combo.

"Want to have a drink and maybe dance?" he asked.

She was about to accept, he could tell. Then she glanced down at her slacks and sweater.

"I'm not dressed for something like that," she said.

"You're perfect. We're going to dance, not put on a fashion show." If he couldn't make love to her, at least he could hold her for a while. Torment himself with her presence, make the day last a little longer.

It was selfish, he knew, but he wanted her to dance with him.

He summoned a bellman over and handed him the bags. "I'm in room 1730," he said, giving the man a tip as well. "We'll be in there," he nodded toward the bar.

The beat was compelling and he swept her onto the dance floor as soon as they reached it. Tucking her in close, he wrapped his arms around her.

"This is nice," she murmured, resting her forehead against his cheek.

"You say that as if it surprises you," he murmured softly, savoring the feel of her against him. She was still too thin, but had begun to fill out a bit. Her hair was soft as silk. He took a deep breath, inhaling the sweet scent of her.

"Being here with you does surprise me," she replied.

He didn't say anything. He wished he could eradicate the past, wished he could make up for all that she'd lost. He raised his hand up her back, squeezing her neck in gentle consolation.

She froze and shrank away from him. He looked into her startled eyes.

"Sorry about that," she said.

"I would never hurt you," he said.

"I know." She took a breath as if schooling herself, and stepped closer.

"What happened?"

For a long moment, he didn't think she would respond. When she did, her voice was so low he almost didn't catch it all.

"A couple of years after I was sent to prison, we got a new guard. One day I sassed him about something and he lit into me, making me an example for all the other inmates. Two other prisoners pulled him off, and soon there was a mob everywhere—guards threatening, prisoners yelling and throwing things at the guards. Almost a riot."

"And you?"

"I missed most of it. One of his fists knocked me out. I was in the hospital for four days."

Jared imagined the horror of the experience and felt another stab of guilt. He silently vowed to make sure Timothy Winters never got out of prison.

"So, you're afraid of men," he said.

"No. Well, a bit. But not you." She tilted her head back until she could see him. "I was at first, but not now."

He lowered his own head until his lips brushed hers. "I feel as if I've been given a precious gift," he said.

He didn't speak again, just moving with her, enjoying the music, alone in a world of two.

The combo segued into song after song. Only when

the musicians took a break did Jared lift his head and look around.

"We can get a drink until they return," he said, spotting an empty table near the dance floor. He seated Susannah near the open space and took the chair opposite.

They ordered, then Susannah glanced around at the other couples. She smiled at Jared. "I'm having fun. Thank you for tonight."

The look on her face caused his heart to race. He didn't want the night to end.

They took a break for as long as the band did, then they were back on the floor.

"Eva is always trying to get me to go dancing. Maybe I'll have to take her up on it. This is fun," she said.

"I can take you dancing if you want. As often as you want."

"What if I said every night?" she teased.

"That would work. I want you, Susannah," he murmured. "Every night would be a bonus."

"Are you sure it's not just the music, the mood?" she asked.

"Oh, I'm sure it's not the music. I've wanted you for a while now. Any chance you want me back?"

"It could change everything between us," she said. But the way she clung gave him hope.

"Change isn't always bad."

"No. But it's sometimes scary."

"I would never do anything to scare you," he said.

She was silent for a long time. "Then, yes," she whispered.

Jared's heart stopped for an instant. Had he heard her correctly?

She tilted her head and smiled at him. "I have only made love with one man, you know, and that was a long time ago. I'm not sure I'm what you really want, but I know you are what I really want."

He covered her mouth with his, unable to wait a second longer to taste her. Crushing her as close as he could, he swayed slowly, deepening the kiss until all he wanted was to whip off the clothes that separated them and feel every inch of her body against him.

Slowly the reality of their location penetrated. He ended the kiss, hating the time it would take to get to his room, hating to part even for a second, but knowing they had to get out of here and go somewhere private.

"Come on," he said, surprised at how husky his voice sounded. She was driving him crazy. He wondered if the hunger would ever be appeased.

SUSANNAH FOLLOWED Jared into the elevator. Had she just committed to spending the night with him? Another couple stepped into the elevator with them, and she kept quiet. But they must have heard her heart pounding. The blood rushing through her ears sounded as loud as Niagara Falls. She clung to his hand, a lifeline to the emotions that swirled. She was going to sleep with this man. They were going to touch each other, kiss each other and make love. She was nervous. But the flare of hope that blossomed wouldn't let her back down. She wanted to affirm life, especially after Timothy's casual dismissal of her life, of her daughter. Jared gave her that hope. He had opened doors for her. Now he would open one more.

Oh God, was she ready?

Her knees threatened to give way. She leaned against the back wall, hoping she didn't sink to a heap on the floor. She could do this. She *wanted* to do this.

Darting a quick glance at Jared, she saw only his profile, the strong line of his jaw. She almost laughed. Neither looked particularly caught up in the heat of passion at the moment. The other couple probably thought they were casual friends.

When they reached their floor, they stepped out.

"Your room or mine?" Jared asked once the elevator doors closed.

"I never thought…I don't care."

"Mine, then. I have a king-size bed."

He unlocked his door and stood aside to allow her to precede him. Susannah's nerves were tightly wound. She turned when he closed the door and encircled his neck with her arms.

"I'm scared silly, but hope a kiss will melt any doubts," she said.

"I aim to please," he said, drawing her into his arms and kissing her.

The passion he unleashed surprised Susannah, but

she reveled in it. Soon their clothing was scattered on the rug as they slowly moved to the bed, kisses and touches arousing every step. Jared yanked back the covers.

"Open the curtains, please," she said as he began to lower her to the mattress. "I don't want the lights on, but I would like to see you."

He pulled open the curtains. Sparkling lights from the city spilled into the room, providing enough illumination to see, providing enough shadows to maintain mystery.

Jared sat on the bed, leaned over her and brushed her hair back from her cheek. "You're sure?"

"Oh yes, Jared, I'm very sure." Reaching up, she pulled him down to her.

CHAPTER TWELVE

NOELLE SLAMMED the door behind her and strode across the foyer to the living room.

"Damn him!" she said, pouring herself a scotch. She'd had enough innuendoes and sly comments tonight to last a lifetime.

She had thought going to the party would be fun. Instead, Judge Creighton had asked her about Jared's sudden interest in adoption processes. Her friend Paulette had asked where Martin was and why she hadn't known he would be gone so long. She'd even had the nerve to suggest Martin was no longer interested in Noelle. And three people had commented on seeing Jared with an unknown blonde recently—Susannah Chapman.

She was the one Jared should be with. She'd waited long enough for him to get over their divorce. She didn't see how his life had improved in the past few months. If anything, it was harder for him to provide child support and run his household. It would make so much sense to recombine homes and get back together.

She paced across the living-room floor. Shrugging

out of her coat, she tossed it to a chair without spilling a drop of her drink.

She went to the phone and dialed his number. She hung up when the answering machine kicked in. She wasn't going to leave any messages.

Maybe he was out with that woman. Had she played into his hands with the injunction?

And where the hell was Martin? He was supposed to go to London for a week. It had been more than twice that, and she hadn't heard from him once.

Suddenly an unexpected fear clutched her. He hadn't tired of her, had he? If Jared didn't come back, she didn't want to be alone. She was fond of Martin. They had a lot in common—the same friends, the same enjoyment of parties, the same lifestyle.

Jared had preferred that house in the woods.

"After all I did for him, he reverts back to nature," she fumed.

She looked at the clock, trying to calculate the time in London. It didn't matter. This was too important to delay.

She dialed the hotel where Martin was staying. He answered on the second ring.

"Did I wake you, darling?" she asked, infusing her voice with enthusiasm, masking the desperate feeling that was gathering strength.

"Noelle. How are you?"

She waited a second. No endearment? Trepidation took hold.

"Fine, darling. Just home from Judge Perle's event.

Half of Denver was there. But with you gone, it wasn't the same. I'm missing you.''

''Things have been busier here than anticipated. Actually, something came up that was totally unexpected.''

''Oh? Do tell me all.'' She perched on the arm of the sofa, swinging her leg, sipping the scotch.

''I was planning to talk to you in the next day or two. I may not be returning to Denver any time soon—except to pack up. I've been offered an assignment here in London.''

Noelle felt the shock to her toes. ''London? Martin, you can't live in London.''

He laughed. ''This is a fantastic opportunity. I'd be a fool to turn it down.''

''But what about me?''

The silence went on too long for Noelle's comfort level. ''I mean, we were seeing each other and all.''

''I asked you to marry me, Noelle. You never gave me an answer. I've been patient, my dear, but even I have a limit. I thought the break might be good for us. See where we stand.''

''I see.''

''This is the first you've called me. I wonder if you even noticed I was gone. How's Jared?''

''I have no idea. He's off somewhere on business this weekend. I have Eric.''

''How's Eric?''

''Fine. I've petitioned for full custody and to keep

Jared away.'' She wasn't sure why she'd told him. She had a feeling he wouldn't approve.

"Why?"

She heard the surprise in his tone. Maybe she'd been impulsive, but she did not want her son around Susannah Chapman. She didn't want Jared around her either, but she had little control over that. Unless this custody situation brought Jared in line.

"Jared is seeing someone I think is unsuitable for Eric. Who knows what he'll expose our son to in the future. I need to take steps to protect Eric.''

"Is it Eric you're thinking about, or yourself?"

Her hand tightened on the phone. "What are you talking about?"

"It's no secret that you want Jared back, though I can't say I understand why. Accept he's moved on, Noelle. Marry me.''

"But you're going to be in London."

"You'd love it here. It's an amazing place, surging with energy and excitement. And only a short hop to the major capitals of Europe. We would have a fabulous life here. And it won't be forever. We could return to Denver when we've had enough.''

"Let me think about it, darling. You've quite caught me by surprise.'' She wanted off the phone. This conversation hadn't gone at all like she expected.

"I'll be back to pack up in another week. I'll need your answer then, Noelle.''

She laughed nervously. "Is that an ultimatum?"

"If you are not going to marry me, then I need to

move on with my life. I don't want to live it alone waiting for you to decide if I'm a better choice than Jared."

"There's no question of that, Martin," she snapped.

It was true, he would be so much better for her. But still she yearned for Jared. Why? Why couldn't she let go?

"I'll call you when I return to Denver," he said.

She sat for a long time holding the dead phone in her hand. Time to make up her mind. What leverage did she have against Jared beside their son Eric?

What had Judge Creighton been talking about? Adoption? Jared wasn't planning to adopt anyone. Why would he be discussing that? It was too late to call anyone tonight.

But tomorrow she'd make some calls and see if she could find out what Jared was doing.

JARED STRODE into his office Monday morning with renewed purpose. The clerk from the county offices had called over the weekend. She had located the records of Susannah's baby. If he'd stop by this morning, she'd give him the information he requested.

He had opened his first brief when Steve Johnson came into the office.

"Want to tell me about your junket this weekend? You took Susannah Chapman to San Francisco to confront Timothy Winters? Are you crazy?" he said without preamble.

Jared rose and faced his boss. "News travels fast," he said. He'd known he'd get some flak from it.

"I got a call from the people in San Francisco. Timothy is being released into the custody of the U.S. Marshals this morning. He'll be in Denver before end of the business day. I'm filing the necessary papers. What the hell were you thinking interrogating him there? And taking that woman with you?"

"I wanted to give Susannah a chance to confront the man. What do you think her chances would be here?" Jared asked evenly.

"His family will hire a battery of attorneys. No one is going to get anywhere near the man before trial," Steve said.

"Right. He set her up to take the fall. She was in prison for eight years for his crime. Don't you think she had the right to face him?"

"Don't let personal feelings interfere with performing your job, Walker. You could have jeopardized the entire case."

"Come off it, Steve, you know that's a bunch of bull. I didn't jeopardize anything. You weren't part of the team that sent her to jail. I was. It's going to be a long time before I forget that."

"Playing knight in shining armor now isn't going to change the past. Stay away from this case, Jared. You and Denning had your chance eight years ago and blew it. I want murder one on this, and don't want to end up plea-bargaining because of some legal screwup."

"I know my job," Jared said.

"Do you? This weekend doesn't prove that. Effective immediately, you're on administrative leave."

"For taking Susannah to see Timothy in another state? He hadn't even been charged at that point," Jared argued.

"For risking the reputation and integrity of this office," Steve shouted.

"For how long?" Jared asked, holding on to his temper by sheer willpower. He wanted to pound something. He had not risked the prosecution of Timothy Winters by allowing Susannah to see him. Steve knew it. He was just putting his ducks in a row before the battle started.

Jared knew there would be a huge brouhaha when the facts emerged. Susannah's release had been front-page news for several days. What would the media do when Timothy returned to Denver?

"I'll tell you when you can come back." Steve stormed from the room.

Jared heard him talking to Rose, ordering her to forward all calls to Ron or Jennifer; requiring the files be transferred to the other A.D.A.s and reminding her of the confidentiality agreement she signed when she started with the department.

A moment later, silence.

"Boss?" Rose stood in the doorway.

"I'll be out of here soon," he said. He felt like a kid who'd been sent to the principal's office.

"Can he do that?" she said.

"As soon as something else hits the news, all will be forgiven and I'll be back." He could challenge Steve's ruling, but that would only get the man's back up. "Let him cool down, and once the media tire of the story, he'll be demanding to know where the depositions I'm doing are," Jared said, trying to lighten the moment.

"Right. And if he doesn't already know you do the work of two, he'll find out pretty quick. Shall I forward calls from the county offices to your home?"

"You are a jewel," Jared said, gathering up a few files and putting them in his briefcase.

"I know." Rose grinned.

He looked up. "I truly do appreciate all you've done since we've worked together."

"Stop, you sound as if you're saying goodbye. Take Eric up to the cabin. He'd love it. And it would probably do you a world of good, too. You don't get enough downtime."

"Hey, he's in kindergarten, did you forget? I can't just haul him out of school on a whim even if my lawyer gets that stupid injunction lifted. Anyway you look at it, things aren't going my way these days."

"But you did right," Rose said. "In all things, you did right."

JARED WOULD HAVE enjoyed his time off a lot more if he could spend it with Susannah. Maybe he would take Rose's advice and spend a few days at the mountain home. He could replenish the wood, fill the cupboards, make sure the propane tank was full.

If Susannah hadn't just started her new job, he might have tried to talk her into playing hooky. Their weekend in San Francisco had been the best hours he'd spent in years.

Waking up with her on Sunday, lazing around in bed, having breakfast, making love again and again. He had wanted to hold on to the day, never let it end.

They had had to run to catch their flight to Denver. And once back in Colorado, she'd insisted he drive her home and leave her at the door.

How was she feeling? Did she have regrets? The thought caused a shaft of pain. He wanted her to be as anxious to see him again as he was to see her. He wanted her to wish to spend time with him, as he did with her. He would never tire of watching the wonder in her eyes, of longing to protect her against the hurts of life. When she'd seen Timothy, and been so bewildered by his callous explanations, Jared had wanted to wring the man's neck for putting her through all she'd endured.

And through it all, the guilt lay heavy for his part. He had been young, untried, but still, he should have done more eight years ago. He resented knowing he was partially to blame for all that had gone wrong. Michael and his quest for reelection had blinded him to standard procedures.

Hindsight was perfect. He wished he could have seen more clearly back then.

The next time he saw her, he'd have news about her daughter. Would it be enough to make up for the wrong?

He swung by the county offices. Helen Baylor was at her desk when he walked into the records department. She looked startled to see him. Recovering swiftly, she rose. "May I help you?" she asked, glancing around. No one seemed to be paying any attention to them. To the others working in the vast room, he was merely another citizen with a routine request.

"I'll be away from the office for a few days. I got your message," he said softly. "What can you tell me?"

She glanced around again.

"Unless you normally do that, I wouldn't," he said. "No one will remember I was here if you treat me like everyone else."

"It could mean my job."

"No one will ever know. Not from me."

She took a slip of paper from her pocket and slid it across the counter. "I've been carrying it with me, feeling it was burning a hole in my pocket," she said nervously. "This is the best I can do."

"Thank you."

"I hope it helps," she said.

He nodded and left, without looking at the paper. Not yet. Helen was a grandmother who had been touched by Susannah's plight. He knew it went against her integrity, but her maternal instincts overruled. Never underestimate the power of motherhood, he thought as he left the building.

Once in his car, he unfolded the slip of paper. *Bob and Rebecca Bradley, 7712 Nicoletti Street, Denver.* There was no phone number, but it would be easy to obtain if needed.

He pulled out a city map and looked up the street. In only moments he was headed in that direction. He could learn a lot about the family from the neighborhood. By afternoon, maybe he could see the little girl return home from school. See enough to reassure Susannah.

NOELLE TOOK a deep breath as the elevator reached the floor she wanted. She had rehearsed what she would say all morning. If Jared ever had a hope of seeing Eric, he had to listen to her. She was not going down without a battle.

Martin's move would provide the final blow. Either Jared started changing toward her, or she would take Eric to London.

"Hello, Rose, is he in?" she walked into the office with as much assurance as she could muster.

"Oh, Mrs. Walker, no." Rose looked up, distressed.

"In court?"

The secretary shook her head. She frowned in indecision. "I guess I can tell you. He's gone home."

"Not sick." Jared had never been sick once since she'd known him.

"No. Wish he were. He's on administrative leave."

"Leave? He didn't mention this to me." Whatever was he doing?

"It was unexpected. And not totally voluntary," Rose said reluctantly.

Noelle stared at her. "What are you talking about?"

Rose looked stricken. "Maybe I've said too much," she said, stacking some papers on her desk, her gaze not meeting Noelle's.

"Jared and I are still close, despite the divorce," Noelle said, keeping her voice modulated. She wanted to grab Rose and shake her. "In fact, I came today to talk to him about…about Susannah Chapman. She's his latest project, you know." Noelle didn't know where that came from, but maybe it would help loosen Rose's tongue.

"That's what got him in hot water with Mr. Johnson. He and Susannah went to San Francisco this weekend to interrogate Timothy Winters."

"Timothy's been found?" Noelle's anger spiked. How could Jared not tell her! And how could he go off for the weekend with Susannah Chapman?

"He'll be back in Denver this afternoon. The extradition papers were faxed over first thing this morning. Mr. Winters was apprehended on Friday night."

"And Jared flew out to interrogate him?"

"Apparently Mr. Johnson wants Jared to stay out of the case, and Jared ignored his orders."

Noelle tried to think. She hadn't expected this.

When Timothy showed up, the press would have a field day. Thank goodness her parents were still in Florida.

With any luck, no one would remember she was a Winters. Rose didn't seem to make the connection.

"I'll catch up with Jared at home, then." Noelle turned and started back toward the elevator, pausing at the doorway as if with an afterthought.

"I don't have Susannah's phone number with me, I was planning to get it from Jared. Do you have it?"

"Sure," Rose said. She flipped to a spot on her Rolodex and copied down a number. Handing the paper to Noelle, she smiled. "I hope Jared gets some rest. He's due in court all next week. I know he'll be back by then."

"I'm sure," Noelle murmured.

When she reached the lobby of the building, she headed for the bank of phones. Dialing the number, she waited impatiently. A man answered.

"Talridge Wholesale Plants."

It wasn't what she'd been expecting. "Talridge Wholesale Plants?"

"Yeah, Pete here. What can I do for you?"

Quickly she tried to think. Rose wouldn't have given her the wrong number. "Is Susannah Chapman there?"

"Yeah, hang on, she's out back. I'll have to go get her."

"No, that's all right. If you could give me directions to your place, I'll stop by when she's finished work. What time would that be?''

''Five o'clock,'' he said.

Noelle wasted no time in driving to the location. She glanced at her watch. It was almost noon. Maybe she could see Susannah on her lunch break. She had no intention of waiting until five.

CHAPTER THIRTEEN

SUSANNAH HAD TROUBLE concentrating. She looked at the seedling she was planting. Had she added the right mixture of soil? She stared at it for a long moment, forgetting all she'd learned. Her mind replayed the weekend. The surreal meeting with Timothy. Jared's attempts to cheer her up.

Their time together in bed.

She flushed thinking about all they'd done. It had been the most exciting night of her life. What she and Shawn had shared so long ago paled in comparison.

And that bothered her.

Shawn had been her love. They had planned to marry, raise a family, grow old together. How could she compare the two?

Of course, she was older now. If not more worldly, at least wiser than the naive young woman at the trial. Today she knew more, would stand up for herself. What doesn't kill you makes you stronger, Marissa always said.

Eva looked at her.

"If I didn't know better, I'd say you were daydreaming. Are you ever going to tell me about your weekend?"

Eva had been pressuring her all morning for details.

"I met with Timothy. It didn't go well. The rest of the weekend was nice."

"Nice? What kind of weekend is that? And in San Francisco? Girl, you should have had a fabulous time, hit every bar in the place, cut loose and had fun."

"I had fun," Susannah said, patting the soil firmly and setting the small container aside. She reached for another.

"Spill!" Eva said.

She looked at Eva and laughed. "Honestly, do I ask you for details?"

"I'd share. You never ask."

"I learned not to ask," Susannah said, remembering the dark days in prison.

"Well, I ask to learn. How will you ever find out things if you don't ask? I'm hurt you don't want to know more about me. I want to be your friend, but you're so tight-lipped. Aren't you at all curious about me? About the other people who work with you? About Jared Walker?"

Susannah looked at her friend, stricken by what she heard. "Do you think that I don't want to be friends because I don't ask questions?" Did Jared think that? She refrained from asking because she didn't want to pry. It wasn't that she wasn't curious.

"What else would I think?" Eva asked.

"That maybe I've lost all social skills I once had. That it would take time to get back into the swing of things?" Susannah suggested. She listened when the others talked, learned things that way. But she didn't feel comfortable asking questions, entering into discussions. Maybe in time.

"Uh-oh, here comes trouble," Susannah said, spotting Noelle Walker wending her way through the rows of plants.

Eva looked up and watched the woman heading their way.

"Wow, now that's style. Who is she?" Eva asked.

"Jared's ex-wife. And she doesn't like me."

"You know her?"

"Not at all, but she thinks I'm a bad influence on their son."

Before Eva could respond, Noelle joined them. She glanced at Eva and the work she was doing. "Could Susannah and I have a moment alone?" she asked, her disdain for their dirty hands evident.

"No," Eva said.

Noelle hadn't expected that. She glared at Eva and turned her eyes to Susannah. "Maybe there is some place we could go to have some privacy."

Susannah dusted off her hands, and wiped them on a towel. "It's almost time for lunch. I'll walk out front with you, if you like."

"You don't have to go with her, Suz," Eva said mildly, her gaze never leaving Noelle.

"I'm sure I can't wait to hear what she has to say," Susannah said. She couldn't imagine what had prompted Noelle to seek her out at work. It must be important—Susannah didn't think Noelle was the type to normally do such things.

When they reached the parking lot, Susannah stopped and looked at Noelle. Her auburn hair was artfully styled as ever and the clothes she wore looked designed just for her. This was the woman Jared had loved enough to marry, to have a child with.

"Jared's been suspended," Noelle said without warning.

"What?"

"That trip you two took over the weekend didn't go over well with his boss. How much more havoc do you plan to wreak in his life before your revenge is satisfied?"

"I'm not after revenge," Susannah said.

"No?" Noelle asked. "Well, you're doing a good job, anyway. I've filed an injunction against him seeing Eric. Now he's suspended from his job. What else do you have planned?"

"Injunction against his seeing Eric? Why?" Could she do that to Jared? If so, why was she telling her?

"Because of the company he's keeping lately, of course," Noelle said.

"I didn't kill anyone, Noelle," she said quietly.

"Maybe not, but being in prison for eight years changes a person."

"So does losing a fiancé and a child."

"A child?" Noelle looked surprised.

"I was pregnant when I went to prison. I gave my baby up for adoption—thinking I was going to be there forever. You have your son—you're lucky. Consider that when judging me. I have nothing.''

''Because of Jared and Michael Denning. You have ample grounds for revenge, I'd say,'' Noelle said.

''Maybe, but that's not my style. Besides, Jared is going to find—'' Susannah stopped. It was none of Noelle Walker's business what Jared was going to do for her.

''Find? What, your child? I doubt it if the adoption records were sealed. Unless he plans to circumvent procedures just like he did with the interview with Timothy. Unlikely. Jared thinks the world of the legal system. This suspension must have hit him hard.''

''As would an injunction forbidding him to see his son. What do you want?'' Susannah didn't want to talk to Noelle anymore. She wanted to call Jared and see if what she was hearing was true.

''I want you to stay away from Jared. He's mine!''

''I thought you two were divorced.''

''Not for long.''

Susannah wondered if it was wishful thinking on Noelle's part, or if they were trying to reconcile. She couldn't believe Jared would have made love to her this past weekend if he were getting back with his ex-wife. But, then, she didn't really know him, did she?

''Don't confuse his guilt with genuine caring. Whatever he's done, it's an attempt to ease his conscience. Tell him you don't need any more help and he'll vanish from your life so fast your head will spin,'' Noelle said, anger lacing her tone. ''And tell him soon, before it's too late.''

''Too late?''

''Just do it!'' Noelle spun around and went to her car.

Susannah watched her drive away, wondering if there was a kernel of truth in her words. Was his attention merely recompense? Was this weekend nothing more than pity for someone locked away for so long?

She didn't want to believe it.

Slowly she returned to the planting area. All thought of eating lunch fled as she considered what Noelle had said.

''So did the wicked witch have anything good to say?'' Eva asked.

''No.''

''You look as if you lost your best friend,'' Eva said.

Susannah looked at her and shook her head. She'd thought Jared was becoming a friend, more than a friend. Now she wasn't sure.

''Don't go by what she said, check it out for yourself,'' Eva suggested.

''Good advice. How did you become so wise?'' Susannah asked.

Eva laughed. ''It's all those parties I go to, it gets easy to spot a phoney a mile away. I could tell you tales that would make your hair curl!''

Susannah tried to listen, but the nagging worry wouldn't let go.

As soon as she was finished work for the day, she headed for the bus. She wanted to get home right away. No time for claustrophobia and getting off the bus to walk a few blocks. The sooner she got home, the sooner she could call Jared.

Though what she'd say when she reached him, she wasn't sure. Hopefully the words would come.

As soon as she stepped off the bus she saw him. He was sitting in his car, parked near the front of the apartment building. He was reading, so he didn't notice her as she approached.

Obviously he wouldn't be here this early if he'd been at work. She knew that much. And he'd changed from his suit into casual clothes. Had Noelle's revelation been true?

She tapped on the window and he looked up.

"Hi," she said when he opened the door.

"Hi, yourself." He checked his watch. "Early bus?"

"No, just rode the entire way. What are you doing here?"

"I came to take you to dinner. And not pizza. I have some good news for you."

"You found my baby," she guessed.

"I did."

"I don't believe it. Tell me!"

"Here?" He looked around as another car sped by.

"I guess not. Come up to the apartment. I can't believe you found her. How did you manage that?"

"Let's go up and I'll tell you everything."

Scarcely containing her impatience, Susannah didn't even notice the closeness of the elevator. As soon as she flung open the apartment door, she turned to him.

"Tell me!" Excitement buzzed through her veins.

"She's a happy little seven-year-old, in second grade. Has one of her permanent front teeth and the other one is coming in. Cute grin."

"You saw her?" Susannah was stunned. It was more than she ever expected. "She's really okay?" Tears welled. Her child was all right.

"Hey, no tears. I'll tell you all I know. It's not much. But I did see her. I heard her calling to friends, and laughing."

"I can't believe it." She sank down on the sofa, unsure how she felt, amazed, grateful, happy.

"Want to go to dinner to celebrate?" Jared asked.

"Tell me everything. How did you find her? Did you really see her? Did she see you? Did you *talk* to her?"

"I called in a few favors and got a line on her adoptive parents. I went to their street, initially just to check out the neighborhood. If it had been in a bad section of town, or something, I might have done more. But it's a nice, middle-class neighborhood. The homes are well kept, lawns neat, and lots of bicycles and other toys giving evidence that a bunch of kids live on that street.''

"So what happened?''

Cocoa came out to see who had arrived. He wove in between Jared's legs and then came to greet Susannah. She couldn't pay attention to the cat, she was focused on every word Jared had to say.

"Want to sit down?'' she asked.

He sat beside her, smiling at the suppressed excitement she couldn't hide. "I got there shortly after noon and was about to drive away when a school bus came down the street. Apparently today was an early release day. I saw her and two friends get off the bus. She headed for the house I'd been watching. She was met at the door by—'' he stopped suddenly.

"By her mother,'' Susannah finished. "You can say it. It's true. I'm only the biological mother. The woman who has loved her all these years is her real mother.'' She rubbed her chest. The ache would never completely go away. But she'd learned to live with it. "I'm so glad she's happy.''

"She seems to be. She has friends, a mother who loves her. I'm sure her father does, too.''

Susannah nodded, leaning back, lost in thought. She still pictured her as an infant. But she was seven now and in second grade. She had friends and rode a school bus. Susannah wondered if she liked school, what her favorite subjects were. Whether her parents were strict but fair, or indulgent.

"Thank you, Jared," she said. Suddenly she remembered Noelle. She sat up and looked at him.

"Did you really get suspended for taking me to San Francisco?"

"Whoa, where did that come from?" he asked.

"Noelle came by work today. She said you'd been suspended. And she told me she filed an injunction to prevent you from seeing Eric because of me."

"Dammit, what is she up to now?"

"Is any of it true?"

Jared rose and paced the small living room. He paused near the window and looked at her. "Steve put me on administrative leave pending the return of Timothy Winters and the flak the office will receive. I knew the risk going in. I wanted you to see Timothy."

"But you didn't want it discovered you took me to San Francisco to interview him, right?" She rose and went to stand near him.

He shrugged. "We didn't break any laws."

"We didn't compromise the case, did we? I want him to get everything he deserves."

"We didn't jeopardize that. But Steve was upset. He wants this to go through perfectly. It's a high-profile case."

"What about Eric?"

"I talked to my attorney today. The injunction has been lifted. It was only instigated by Noelle for not getting her way. I'm moving ahead with plans to petition for joint custody. Which means I will get Eric at least half the time.''

''So her coming to see me today was some kind of bluff?''

''No, she's still trying to call the shots.''

''But you and she aren't getting back together any time soon?''

He looked startled, turning to hold her eyes. ''Another comment from Noelle?''

Susannah nodded, feeling the relief spread when he shook his head.

''No, we are not getting back together. How could you think that after last weekend?'' he asked softly.

''I didn't want to, but she sure came across as certain.''

''We will always have a connection with Eric. But our marriage ended.''

''Do I have time for a quick shower before we go to dinner?'' Susannah asked.

''Take your time. Do you want Chinese? I know a nice place nearby.''

''Sounds good.''

While in the shower, Susannah vowed she would take Eva's advice and question Jared to her heart's content. If he didn't want her to know something, he could tell her. Her curiosity was bubbling over. She wanted to know *everything!*

She had to reach out and learn to trust again or she would be stuck in a prison of her own making. She'd been closer to Jared last weekend than she'd been to anyone, even Shawn.

Twenty minutes later she faced herself in the mirror. Tilting her chin, she smiled when she remembered Jared had seen her daughter. He'd risked a lot to give her peace of mind. She would forever be grateful. But she had a dozen more questions she hoped he could answer.

"Ready?" He rose when she came into the living room.

"Yes. And starved." She pushed Noelle's words to the back of her mind. She would not let the woman ruin their evening. Or the possibility of any future they might have.

The mere thought scared her, but she pushed that away, too. Tonight was hers.

As soon as they ordered, she put her new vow into action. "Tell me about being suspended."

"Administrative leave."

"Is that common?"

He looked into her eyes. "No. But nothing to worry about."

"Could you get fired over this?"

"Not likely."

"But possible."

"No."

"When are you going to see Eric again?"

"Soon. I'm getting him Wednesday evening to make up for missing this weekend. I'm going to see him perform in a school play about Thanksgiving, then he's coming home with me. I think he's playing an Indian.''

"Not a pilgrim?"

"If I understood him correctly, he's an Indian, but not the chief.''

"Is that distinction important?"

"Not to him. Do you want to come?"

"I'd love to. Do you go to all his school events?"

"I want to, but we're just starting.''

"My father never made it to mine. The military always came first.''

"My father didn't make it either. The bottle came first.''

She blinked. His father was an alcoholic? Impulsively she reached out and squeezed his hand. "I'm sorry,'' she said.

His hand turned, grasped hers firmly, his thumb rubbing lazily against her wrist. "I was, too, growing up. I've come to accept it now.''

"Still, it's hard, isn't it? I always felt like I was the only child who didn't have someone who cared enough to come.''

"That's why I want to go to all of Eric's events. So far that's only been preschool graduation and Back-To-School Night in September. But I plan to make them all.''

"Will Noelle be there?"

"I don't know.''

"Tell me about growing up in one place your

whole life. I moved every two to three years. There's no place to call home," she said, not wanting to spend their time together talking about Noelle.

Instead, she wanted to know every detail, every happy moment, and every sad one of Jared's life. When his mother died, and how he coped with his father's situation. Who his friends had been, and what they shared in common. Why he'd chosen law.

It was as if she'd opened the floodgates. He spoke quietly, but succinctly, telling her what she wanted to know, and when he didn't offer enough she prompted him for more. Their meal arrived and they shared the different plates of Chinese food, commenting from time to time on how delicious it was.

Susannah brought the topic back to his life every time he flagged.

"So that's why you went into law," she said after he related a story of a neighbor who had been cheated by the landlord.

"One reason. I wanted justice. As I got into it, I decided criminal law was stronger. I could put away serious criminals and not just petty landlords who preyed on the downtrodden."

"You're a white knight. I would never have thought it eight years ago," she said softly.

"Slightly tarnished, if my track record is examined closely. I'm not perfect as you well know."

"But that's in the past. Finding out about my daughter makes up for everything." She beamed at him. "Tell me again what she looked like."

He told her of the long dark hair, slender body, cute grin. How she'd yelled to her friends long after they were close enough to really hear each other.

His dark eyes held hers when he finished. She felt as if he were searching for something. Absolution? Forgiveness?

WHEN THE FORTUNE COOKIES arrived, Susannah broke hers open and read it, looking up to find his gaze once again on hers.

"Read it aloud," he invited.

"The brave make their own fortune." She wrinkled her nose. "I would have wished for something more like, a long journey awaits you."

"And where would you go?"

She thought about it a moment, then smiled shyly. "San Francisco. I had a great time there."

"We can have a great time right here in Denver."

"Read yours."

Jared broke the cookie and took the slip of paper out to read. "Truth will triumph."

"Gee, that's wisdom for you," Susannah teased. "Is that the best they can do?"

"Apparently. Are you ready to go?"

She nodded.

Once outside Susannah took a deep breath. She'd done fine in the restaurant sitting by the window. She wondered if she would always be uncomfortable being closed in, of feeling confined even in spacious rooms. At least she now had the freedom to walk away if things became too intense.

Jared walked beside her to the car. She hesitated a moment, then turned to him.

"I'm sorry, I was just congratulating myself for doing so well in the restaurant, and now find I just can't get in the car."

He leaned against the door and reached out to push a strand of hair from the edge of her eye. The breeze blew it into disarray.

"Want to walk home? It's only about twenty blocks."

"What about your car?"

"I'll walk back when I leave."

"That's silly. Just give me a minute."

"Have you thought about seeing someone about this?" he asked.

"A shrink, you mean?"

"A counselor who could help you."

"I'll consider it, once I get some money. I'm making minimum wage, no health care benefits and I'm living in a borrowed apartment for two months. Seeing someone to help with claustrophobia is low on my list right now."

"I could—"

She held up her hand. "No, don't even go there. You have done more for me than anyone could have expected. I will not take any more."

He took her hand and kissed the palm. "We could discuss this in the warmth of your borrowed apartment, if you're inviting me back.'' Linking his fingers with hers, he turned.

"What are you doing?" she asked as he began to walk away from the car.

"Walking you home."

"But the car."

"It'll be safe enough here. Come on."

Susannah gave in. It was easier than arguing when she still didn't feel comfortable enough to get into the vehicle. Maybe he was right, she needed to do something to work through this fear of confinement.

Or maybe things would work out one day once she accepted she was truly free and wouldn't be going back to jail.

When they reached her apartment, Jared called to check his messages. She prepared coffee for them, wondering if there was a problem by the expression on his face. He must have had a lot of messages, because he listened for a long time.

She took her cup on the small patio, leaving the door cracked behind her. When she stood against the railing, she felt as if she were almost floating on air. She could lean out just far enough not to see the apartment building from her peripheral vision. It was as if she were an eagle who could fly anywhere at a moment's notice. Here is where she felt free.

"Sorry about that. I didn't realize there would be so many messages. I should have though—Timothy Winters returned to Denver today."

"Reporters?" she asked, turning reluctantly. She

wasn't quite ready to go inside, yet it was getting colder by the moment.

"Reporters, the attorney for the defendant and Noelle. You never did tell me what she wanted."

"She was warning me away from you," Susannah said.

He took a deep breath. "She has been pampered all her life. And my leaving hurt her pride. She'd like to get back together, but that's not going to happen. She's a party girl from way back. We went out three and four times a week. If I'd call to say I had to work late on a case, she'd get furious. Reasoning didn't work well. She wanted to party and accepted invitations time and again for us even when she knew I was too busy. To her, being with other people, entertaining, or being entertained is what life is all about."

"She must have been proud of your work, your contribution."

He looked at her oddly, as if finding it difficult to see her in the dim light coming from inside. "Can you say you are?"

"I blame Michael Denning and Timothy. You were there, but too green to do anything but be a yes-man."

Jared winced. "Don't pull your punches."

"But you've matured, and have strong principles that anyone would be proud of. Hearing you talk tonight, I realized justice is important to you and to who you are. So, yes, I guess I am proud of what you do."

He stepped closer and took her cup, placing it on the railing. Drawing her closer, he kissed her.

The panic didn't come. Instead, Susannah felt as if she were soaring. Encircling his neck with her arms, she pressed herself against him, delighting in the feel of his strong body against hers, the sense of freedom. The kiss deepened and coherent thought fled. Only feelings remained, glorious sensations that pulsed and swept through her like the surging sea.

She could spend the rest of her life like this.

"Maybe we should get a pup tent and find a spot in a field," he said, trailing kisses along her jaw, down to the rapid pulse point at the base of her throat.

"I have a perfectly good bed."

"But we start outside in the cold often enough."

"At the cabin once, and that was just a kiss."

"Just a kiss? Here I thought I wasn't the only one hearing bells."

She laughed softly. "Hearing bells? I doubt it. But you're right, it wasn't just a kiss. It was spectacular."

"Ah, and tonight?"

"Are we rating them?"

"Unless you have a better idea?"

"As I said, there's a perfectly good bed inside."

He pulled back a little to look at her. "Are you ready to go inside?"

She snuggled closer and nodded. Her heart filled with his thoughtfulness. He probably had never dated anyone who couldn't stay long inside, was fearful of big men, didn't liked closed-in spaces.

Surely the fact that he was with her had to mean more than mere atonement for a wrong done so long ago.

CHAPTER FOURTEEN

ON WEDNESDAY Susannah asked to work through lunch so she could take off early. Pete had no problem with her request, once he knew it was to see a child's play.

"I have three grandkids. I take off myself from time to time. Two are in the band in high school. The third is the star of his Little League team. You can see one of his games come spring, if you'd like," he said.

"I'd like that," she said. Eva was right. It was time to open up to others, forge trust in relationships. Pete had extended the hand of friendship—she wouldn't forget that.

Jared picked her up, Eric already in the car.

"Hi, Susannah. I'm going to be an Indian," he said in greeting.

"So I hear. I can't wait to see your play. Have you been practicing?"

Eric nodded emphatically. "I have words to say and everything. But I don't get to carry a bow and arrow. Teacher said this was a feast so Indians didn't take weapons."

"I'm sure she's right. When you go to a party, you don't take things like that."

"Is that what a feast is, a party?" Eric asked.

"Sure is. And Thanksgiving was one of the first big parties in America, before it was even America."

"Huh?"

"I don't think they've progressed enough to know what you're talking about," Jared said with a smile as he drove through the city streets.

"That's my school," Eric said excitedly.

Jared drove into the parking lot which was already filling up with cars. The kindergarten class was not the only class giving a performance for family and friends.

He delivered his son to the teacher while Susannah waited in the hall. She looked at the bulletin boards, the artwork done by students, photos of honor roll recipients. The children in those photos looked to be the fifth or sixth graders.

A pang struck her. If things had been different, she'd be a part of a school like this. She might even have been coordinating a Thanksgiving event with her students. She had been so enthusiastic when she'd done her student teaching. Young children loved to learn, and she'd felt she'd made a difference.

All gone now. Too much had happened for her to regain that enthusiastic joy in the future.

Was her daughter's school similar to this one? Would she be on the honor roll some day?

"Sorry, I got waylaid by a home-room mother. She

said something about bringing cupcakes to the class parties, but then we heard that the play is about to start,'' Jared said, joining her in front of the bulletin board.

Entering the classroom a moment later, Susannah stopped abruptly. It was already crowded with parents and siblings. The small chairs were lined up theater style and most were occupied. She felt a flare of panic. How could she not have thought this through? There were too many people, packed too close together—

''Come on, there's space near the windows. We'll stand.'' Jared didn't wait to hear her answer, merely took her hand and led her to a spot where there was more space. But the afternoon was waning. It would be dark soon and any feeling of relief from the windows would be lost when they reflected back the classroom lights.

She took a deep breath. She would be fine, she told herself, focusing on the front of the room, trying to ignore the people who still crowded in. How many relatives could a class of kindergartners have?

''You holding on?'' Jared asked as the boys and girls trooped in.

She nodded, picking out Eric immediately. She smiled at the boy and concentrated on watching him, ignoring the clamoring sensations that made her want to flee.

The play was funny, and enthusiastically performed. The Indians seemed to have the best time, and Susannah laughed aloud a couple of times at their antics, and the way they garbled their lines. No one minded, however.

As soon as the play was over, the teacher invited everyone to stay for refreshments. Jared encircled Susannah's shoulders and headed for the door. "You can wait outside while I find Eric. We're not staying."

"Oh, there you are, Mr. Walker," a young woman said as they approached the door. She smiled at Susannah.

"Mrs. Walker?"

"Susannah Chapman. And you are— I'm sorry I've forgotten your name," Jared said.

"Betty Cummings," she said, holding out her hand to Susannah with a smile. "I spoke to Mr. Walker earlier reminding him we all need to do our bit to help at parties. The Christmas party will be the last day of school. We are hoping for some contribution from all the children."

"I'm sure cupcakes would be easy enough to send," Susannah said. "Count on him for two dozen."

"How delightful," Betty said. "I'll note that down. See you later." She walked to another set of parents and Susannah heard her spiel as she and Jared escaped to the hallway.

"If two dozen cupcakes are required, I'll need some help," he said.

"How hard can that be?"

"I have no idea. I've never made cupcakes."

She frowned. It had been years, of course, since she had made any. But Shawn had enjoyed them. Just the right size to eat without having to cut a slice of cake, he'd always said.

"Fine, we'll do it together."

"I'll hold you to that. Can you find the car? I'll get Eric and we'll join you. I thought we'd have dinner at the cabin. Okay with you?"

"You didn't mention that. Are we coming back tonight? I have work tomorrow."

"If it's a problem, we can stay in Denver. But I'll have you back for work."

"I have nothing to wear tomorrow."

"So we'll swing by your place before we go." He fished out his keys and handed them to her. "Wait in the car, or by it if you're not ready to get inside."

As he turned away another couple came from the room.

"Weren't they darling?" the woman asked.

Susannah nodded. "The best play I've seen," she said.

"First time, I bet," the man said. "This is our third kid—I've almost memorized the play."

"Which one was yours?" the woman asked.

"Eric Walker, one of the Indians." He wasn't hers exactly, but he was the student she'd come to see. She didn't mind being linked that way. It was almost as if she were part of the family.

"Julia Baker is ours, one of the pilgrims. The one

who kept eating when she should have been saying her lines. You'd think we didn't feed her enough," the woman said.

When they reached the parking lot they turned in the opposite direction to Susannah, wishing her a happy Thanksgiving.

The drive to the mountains went without incident, probably because Eric talked nonstop and Susannah didn't have a moment to dwell on feeling confined.

Dinner was fun, grilled cheese sandwiches and soup. Once Eric had been put to bed, Jared and Susannah put on their jackets and went out on the deck to enjoy the last of the evening.

"He did so well," she said with a feeling of pride in Eric's accomplishments.

"He won't win any Oscars, but he did fine, didn't he?"

"Life is more than winning awards. He had fun, learned something new and gave a lot of enjoyment to all who saw him tonight. I'm surprised Noelle didn't come."

"I was, too, truth to tell. She's a good mother. But she is also a poor loser and because I got her injunction lifted, she sees it as a loss. She didn't anticipate my petitioning for joint custody."

"Maybe she feels threatened by the change," she suggested.

"She'll always be his mother. No one can take that place."

Susannah swallowed hard. It was true.

"Jared, can you take me to see my little girl?"

JARED FELT as if he'd been blindsided. He had not anticipated that. Which had been stupid on his part. A child was an important part of a woman's life, of any parent's life. He should have known she'd want more than his assurances her daughter was happy.

"I thought you said once you knew she was happy, you'd be content."

"I thought I would. But you've seen her. Heard her laugh. I'm so jealous. I want to see her. Just once. I won't interfere with her life, I promise. But just to see her, is that so much to ask?"

"Susannah, I already broke a dozen rules and regulations getting that address, going to check up on her myself. I can't give you that information. It goes against all the laws about adoption."

"I haven't seen her since she was two hours old. I have never forgotten her for a single moment since. Now I'm free. I can't ever be her mother, I know that. But just to see her— Oh, Jared, it would mean the world to me."

He felt torn. He knew she longed to see her daughter. But he was an officer of the court. While bending the laws was not strictly legal, he'd done no harm so far. Could he bend the rules enough to take her to see the child? He was sworn to uphold the law. But what of justice?

"If you like, I'll promise to leave Denver once I've seen her," she said quietly.

"What? Where did that come from?" He spun around to look at her.

"There's nothing to hold me here. Eva is my only friend. When my cell mate, Marissa, gets out, I thought we might travel south. Go some place warmer and start over."

"I'm your friend," he said. The thought of her leaving left him shaken. He had been thinking they had something growing, but if she could so casually talk about leaving, it had to be all one-sided.

"Thank you."

"Thank you?"

"For being my friend." She came to stand beside him, and leaned against him. "I don't have many, you know. I cherish each one."

He liked the sound of cherished. Was it enough to build on?

"Ready to go inside?" he asked. He wanted to talk to her about this foolish idea.

"No, but you can go ahead. Don't stay out for me."

"You can sit by a window."

"Nothing against your wonderful house, but the windows are a little small. And I can't see anything outside when it's dark. Standing here, the starlight illuminates the trees. I know I'm free."

"I have outside lights, want me to turn them on?"

"I'm fine just like this. It's so peaceful and quiet. You are lucky to have this place, Jared. If it were mine, I'd never leave it."

Jared thought about living permanently at the mountain house. Eric would love living here. If Jared was successful in gaining joint custody, he'd rather raise his son here than in the high-rise apartment. And he was starting to envision Susannah as an integral part of that arrangement.

"Think on what I asked, Jared. I just want to see her," she said.

"And if I don't agree?"

She shrugged. "Then I don't get to see her. I'm not going to pester you every time we meet."

"But you'll go ahead with plans to move?"

"I don't know. I'm not sure yet what I want to do."

An unsatisfactory answer, but one he'd have to live with for the moment.

It wasn't as if he were asking her to make a commitment to him. He wasn't ready for such a step either. How could he trust his feelings in the matter? He'd thought he'd loved Noelle, and those feelings hadn't lasted. They had not been deep enough to weather the differences in their lifestyles.

He wasn't even sure he knew Susannah's lifestyle, but he felt a connection with her he hadn't felt with Noelle.

Or was it only guilt, trying to right an old wrong?

Steve had ended the administrative leave once he'd realized the defendant's attorney was not going to make an issue of Jared's interview with Timothy Winters in San Francisco. Work demanded a lot of attention, even though he was kept out of the loop on the Winters case. According to Steve, Jared had had his shot at justice, now someone else would see to it.

Was that what he was doing with Susannah?

He hated thinking that might be the case. How would he ever know if he didn't take a step beyond what was comfortable and ask her to stay with him. Marry him?

"I'm getting cold, I think I'll go to bed now. Good night," she said before he could continue the thought.

So much for asking her to marry him. It didn't look as if she planned to share his bed tonight, either. Where was this relationship going?

Where, exactly, did he want it to go?

SUSANNAH SPENT Thanksgiving with Eva. The two of them had as much fun as they'd had on their shopping day. Eva was a great cook, and Susannah enjoyed the meal, and the leftovers Eva insisted she take.

Jared had mentioned Thanksgiving, telling her he had already committed to spending it with Noelle and Eric. She could understand the little boy celebrating his holidays with both parents, but maybe Jared was sending Noelle mixed messages if he shared holidays with her.

Still, the day proved wonderful. She had Friday off and did something she never thought she would do—voluntarily returned to the Colorado State Prison for Women. She visited with Marissa, catching her up on all her news, and making plans. Marissa would be out early in the new year, and Susannah hoped to be able to get an apartment they could share—if they decided to remain in Denver.

Without any ties, maybe it would be better to settle far away. She wouldn't wonder every time she saw a child with long brown hair if it were her daughter. Wouldn't be afraid things would reverse themselves somehow and she'd wind up back in prison.

But she clung to the hope that Jared was coming to care for her as she was for him. He was different from Shawn, and at one time she'd thought Shawn the love of her life. But maybe a woman could have two loves, each important, each different.

Jared called, took her to dinner, shared weekends with her and Eric. But they didn't seem to be moving beyond friendship. He made no further move to take her to bed, not that she expected him to with a young child present. But it confused her and left her wondering.

It was late one Wednesday afternoon when he called her at work.

"I'll be leaving for home soon, couldn't this wait until then?" she asked, feeling awkward to be taking a personal call at work.

"It couldn't wait. I'll pick you up after work. If I'm a few minutes late, wait. Don't take the bus."

"Fine. I'll wait out front." He had picked her up a couple of times after work. They'd grabbed a quick meal and then returned to her apartment, usually to a long after-dinner walk. Sometimes to sit on the cold balcony and talk.

When Jared's car slid to a stop a little after five, Susannah hopped in. She hadn't seen him since the past Sunday afternoon, and was pleased he wanted to see her again midweek.

He pulled away and headed toward her apartment.

"What's up?" she asked. He'd made no mention of dinner.

"Saturday you and I are going to meet your daughter," he said.

"What?"

"I've arranged it with her parents. Not without some reluctance on their part. But her mother, Rebecca, said she knew how you felt and wanted to reassure you. Her husband isn't so amenable, but did agree. They will call the shots, but you get to meet her."

She stared out the window, dumbfounded. *She was going to meet her daughter.* Actually speak to her.

To see her, hear her voice, know she was healthy and happy, it was more than she'd ever dreamed of.

"Thank you, Jared," she said simply. The magnitude of the gesture was overwhelming. She knew his finding out their address had been violating the law. To actually take her there was monumental.

"What time Saturday? What shall I wear? I shouldn't get too dressed up, should I? But I want to make a nice impression on both the parents and her. What will I say? Are they telling her who I am?"

"They are not telling her who you are. You'll get to meet her, but as a passing acquaintance of her parents. This is a one-off deal, you are not to contact them again, nor go to their home, nor to her school. I want your promise on that, Susannah."

"I promise." She was going to see her baby once more. She could hardly wait.

SATURDAY, Jared picked her up at ten. She hadn't slept more than a few hours at a time since she heard the news. Dressing carefully, Susannah rehearsed all she wanted to say. She hoped she wouldn't be too nervous or tongue-tied to speak. Her stomach felt like it was tied in knots, her heart careened out of control. Still, when she gazed at herself in the mirror, she didn't see the turmoil. Just the anticipation and excitement.

She clutched her purse tightly as Jared drove across town. She made no effort to memorize where they were going. She wasn't familiar with Denver and knew she wouldn't be able to find the place again. Not that she would try. She'd given her word.

At the house, Jared rang the bell and a short woman with dark hair opened the door.

"Rebecca, this is Susannah Chapman."

"Come in."

Jared introduced Susannah to Bob, being careful not to give out the man's last name.

Susannah could tell Bob was not in favor of this

meeting. She wished she could reassure him, but only time would do that.

"Thank you so much for agreeing to this," she said when they all sat down. "Jared said he explained everything. How I came to give her up and all."

"Yes. We are grateful to have her. She is our precious daughter and we love her as much as if she'd been born to us. We got her when she was only three days old, and have taken such loving care of her," Rebecca said.

Susannah reached into her purse and drew out two envelopes. She handed them to Rebecca.

"I wrote these after Jared told me of the meeting. The thick one has all the history I could remember of my family and Shawn's. Medical information, church background, anything I thought you might want to know some day. Our families were healthy, though both of us lost our parents before we graduated from college. But neither of us have any background of chronic illness."

"And the second envelope?" Bob asked gruffly.

"It's a letter to my daughter. I didn't seal it, so you can read it if you like. I was hoping you'd give it to her sometime in the future, if she ever asks about me. She knows she's adopted, doesn't she?" Susannah wasn't sure if this was part of the deal, but it couldn't hurt to try.

"She knows, and that we love her. She doesn't know about what happened," Rebecca said, fingering the envelope. "If she asks when she's older, I'll see she gets the letter."

"Thank you." Susannah's heart was pounding. How long before her precious baby came into the room?

"I didn't know how to address it, so I addressed it to Annie, that was Shawn's mother's name and I called her that until they took her away."

Rebecca looked at her husband. "We named her Molly, for my husband's grandmother," she said gently.

Susannah caught back tears. Of course her daughter wouldn't have had the name she'd given her. In the future, she'd no longer think of her as Annie. How hard would that be?

"Why don't you call Molly, Bob." When he left, Rebecca said, "She and her friend Brittany are playing in her room. We thought we'd just introduce you as people we know passing through Denver who stopped to visit."

"However you wish to handle it is fine with me. Thank you again, I'm so grateful." Susannah looked toward the archway from the hall, listening for sounds of her coming.

Bob stepped into the room, and a little girl followed him, holding a doll. She looked at her mother and smiled, then looked curiously at Susannah and Jared.

"Oh my God, she looks just like Shawn," Susannah whispered. Her heart clutched. The rich chestnut hair was the color Shawn's had been. Her eyes were dark. She even had a slight cleft in her chin, so reminiscent of the man she'd once loved. Yet she was her own person, as well.

Eagerly Susannah memorized each feature. She longed to take her in her arms and hold her close. Tell her how much she missed her. Tell her how much her daddy would have loved her. They had all missed out.

Except Molly. She had a set of loving parents. It was obvious by the looks they shared.

"Honey, I wanted you to meet Susannah and Jared. They stopped by for a short visit and wanted to see you."

"Hello, Molly," Susannah said, blinking back tears. She wouldn't give way. Not in front of her daughter. "I last saw you when you were a tiny baby. You've grown up. How pretty you are."

"I'm seven."

"Yes, I know. And in second grade, aren't you? Do you like school?"

"It's okay. Brittany and I get to sit next to each other, and play at recess."

"It's nice to have a special friend."

Jared's hand covered hers, and she gripped it as though it was a lifeline. This was so hard. She wanted to sweep the child up and run away with her. She wanted all the days and weeks and years lost to her. Wanted to see her smile for the first time, to take her first step, hear her first word. All lost forever.

"Can I go now?" Molly asked her mother.

"Sure. When our guests leave, I'll fix you and Brittany lunch."

"Bye, nice to meet you," Molly said with a quick smile before she dashed away.

Tears fell despite her best efforts. Jared handed her a handkerchief with his free hand, his other one still firmly wrapped around hers.

"Thank you," Susannah said, fumbling with the white cloth. She tried to dry her eyes, but felt as if she was about to completely lose it. "I think we should go."

He rose, pulling her up with him. "Thank you both, again. It meant a great deal as you can see."

"We'll take care of your baby," Rebecca said. She handed Susannah a small album. "I made you a baby book, so you can see how she fared until now. If you like, I'll send pictures from time to time, through Jared's office?"

Susannah gave a sob and nodded. "Thank you."

Jared thanked them for their thoughtfulness and compassion in allowing Susannah to see their daughter. He hustled her to the car. Her tears couldn't be held back.

Once inside the vehicle, he turned and drew her into his arms.

"Cry it out, sweetheart. I know that was hard. But you saw, she's happy and well adjusted. She has friends, finds school okay and has parents who adore her. Put your worries to rest."

Susannah cried for almost ten minutes, then slowly

sat back. "I've ruined your shirt, made an idiot of myself and I'm exhausted. But isn't she beautiful?"

"She is a very pretty little girl. She'll grow up to be gorgeous."

"They were kind to let me come, weren't they?"

"More so than most might have been."

She traced a finger over the album. "And to give me this. They took such a risk letting me see her."

"One mother's empathy to another," he said, moving to start the car.

"I will always miss her, but I know she is loved and happy. That helps. Thank you, Jared."

"What next?"

"Take me home, I guess," she said. She longed to open the album, see every picture Rebecca had shared with her. For a little while, she'd have her daughter.

"I'm picking Eric up at one. Spend the weekend with us," Jared invited.

"At the cabin?"

"No. Here in Denver. We'll go to the natural history museum this afternoon, and tomorrow take in a movie. You haven't lived if you haven't seen a Disney movie with a couple of hundred screaming kids."

She shook her head. "I guess not, but time I did." She hugged the album to her chest and gazed sightlessly out the window. "It went by too fast," she said. "Do you think she'll ever remember me? Ever want to know me?"

"I can't guess the future," Jared said, slowing as

they neared her apartment. "If she does, I expect her parents would not stand in her way."

"They'll always be her parents. But I would like her to know, one day, why I wasn't able to raise her." She looked up as he stopped in front of her building. "I hope she'll get to read my letter sometime."

"I'll drop you and go get Eric. We'll be back soon."

"I could go with you," she said, feeling guilty wanting to be by herself the first time she looked through the album.

"I thought you might wish to see the album by yourself. Look at it, enjoy it, and we'll be back in about an hour."

She leaned over and kissed him lightly. "I'll be ready."

Scrambling out of the car, she headed inside, anticipation building once again at the thought of seeing the first seven years of Molly's life through pictures.

Slowly she opened to the first page. The tiny baby she remembered was there, in a pretty pink blanket. There were photos with both Rebecca and Bob, their own happiness shining in the pictures. Slowly her daughter grew. Rebecca had jotted notes beside each photo: first step, first birthday, though the frosting smeared over Molly's face would have given Susannah enough of a clue. The final page had a copy of her second-grade school picture.

Lovingly, Susannah traced her daughter's face with

her finger. She would always be grateful for today. And it was Jared who had made it possible.

She looked at her clock. He and Eric would be here soon. She went to wash her face and brush her hair. Only slightly swollen eyes gave a hint of her bout with tears. But Eric wouldn't notice. He'd be too caught up with whatever was going on, living in the moment, enjoying every aspect of life.

She could do worse than to take lessons from a five-year-old. Live in the moment, enjoy every second.

She went downstairs to wait for them outside. It was a cold, clear day, the sun giving an illusion of warmth. But the cool air felt good. She'd have to give a lot of thought to where to live. If it was some warm locale, she could do a lot of living outdoors, have the windows open. Not feel so closed in.

But leaving Jared? She didn't think she could do that. He'd filled such a big part of her life since she'd gotten out, she had trouble imaging life without him.

Eric greeted her exuberantly as always when she got into the car. "Daddy said we were going to get you. I said you should have come with him, but then Mommy asked where we were going and what we were going to do and with who. Mommies have to make sure you mind your manners and don't play with children who aren't suitable," he said.

"That's an important job your mommy has," Susannah said. Suddenly another reason for Jared's dropping her off earlier sprang to mind. Had he not wanted her in the car when he went to Noelle's?

CHAPTER FIFTEEN

"TODAY'S THE ARRAIGNMENT, isn't it?" Eva asked on Monday morning.

Susannah nodded, concentrating on her task. She didn't want to talk to anyone today. The weekend had been trying. First the joy of seeing her daughter for the second time in her life.

And then the uncertainties and fears she had that Jared was only seeing her to atone for his part in her wrongful conviction.

She didn't want that. For a while she thought they might be putting the past behind them. That they might have a chance at a future together.

But that was before he made sure she never connected with Noelle when he picked up Eric and dropped him off. That they went to an out-of-the-way spot for dinner so no one he knew could see them.

"Why aren't you there?" Eva asked, not to be put off.

Susannah looked at her friend. "Because I don't want to take a day off work."

"Bull. Try another."

Susannah dusted the soil from her hands and nodded. "You're right. The real reason is that I didn't think I could trust myself not to make a scene. I'm still so angry and frustrated that everything happened as it did. But mostly that Timothy, who I thought was a friend, could let me go to jail for life. If those people hadn't spotted him in San Francisco, I'd still be in prison and he'd still be living life to the fullest."

"All the more reason, I'd think, to be there during the trial. See that justice is done. And gloat when it is," Eva said.

"I'm being called as a witness at the trial. I talked to Pete and he said I could have the time—no pay, of course." Susannah didn't care about that. She just wanted justice. She wanted the world to know not only that she was innocent, but who was guilty.

"Go now, don't wait until the trial. It'll help with closure," Eva urged.

"Do you think?"

"Oh, yeah, I sure do. Wish I could go and throw rotten eggs or something," Eva said strongly.

Susannah laughed. "That would be a sight. Timothy with rotten eggs dripping off him."

"Serve him right. Maybe tomatoes, too. Go, you need to see this through, and there's no reason he shouldn't have to face you. I think a public apology is the least he should do. Besides, someone has to make sure he doesn't cop a plea, or something."

"Jared promised there would be no plea bargain. Besides, this is only the arraignment, to bind him over for trial." She knew more about the entire process than she ever wanted to know.

"Doesn't matter. You need to see every step is carried out as it should be."

Susannah nodded. "I'll go." She checked her watch. It was still early morning. But by the time she got home, changed and to the courthouse, the proceedings would surely have started. She remembered it didn't take long for an arraignment hearing. It wasn't like it was the actual trial.

WHEN SHE ARRIVED at the courthouse it was almost eleven. She had to ask directions to the appropriate courtroom. Walking along the wide corridors, she felt a shiver of apprehension. It was impossible to keep from remembering her trial.

Slipping into the courtroom quietly, she noticed Steve Johnson was already talking to the judge, presenting the state's case. She took a seat in the back, glancing around.

Jared was seated in the front row beside Noelle. Two other suit-clad men were with them, relatives? Or legal representation?

There were a few spectators, but most of the seats near the front were filled with reporters rapidly scribbling notes. Obviously the judge had banned photographs as the cameras hung unused around necks.

Steve made a good case for holding Timothy Winters over for trial for first-degree murder. He and Todd had been roommates, who fought constantly. Friends attested they had not seen nor heard from Todd since the murder. The thinking had been he'd been too distraught from Timothy's death to stay in Denver. In light of Timothy being alive, the testimony of Todd's being missing was damning.

When Timothy's lawyer spoke, the reporters seemed to inch closer. But the defense attorney had little effect.

The judge ruled to hold the prisoner for trial. Bail denied. Timothy had already proved a flight risk.

Susannah breathed a sigh of relief at that ruling. At least he would still be here for trial.

When the judge dismissed the court, the reporters surged forward, clamoring for answers from Timothy, his attorney, the district attorney. Some focused on Jared and Noelle, firing questions almost nonstop. Who could sort them out to answer?

Susannah shrank back in her chair. She had forgotten about the media that was sure to cover this event. Taking a deep breath, she got up and quickly slipped from the courtroom, hoping no one recognized her.

The hall was jammed and she moved behind one of the tall pillars that supported the upper floors.

From her hiding spot, Susannah could see Jared and Noelle as they came out of the courtroom with reporters almost surrounding them. They moved slowly toward the elevators at the end of the corridor.

"No comment." She recognized Jared's deep voice.

"I have nothing to say," Noelle added, clinging to Jared as they tried to move through the horde of reporters snapping questions. Photos were obviously permitted here. Flashes went off with great regularity.

"Is there any truth to the rumor you two are getting back together?" one reporter asked. "Is this family crisis bringing you together?" another asked.

Susannah caught her breath. She hadn't heard any rumors like that. Jared had been spending time with her.

"No comment," Jared snapped.

"We may have had our differences in the past," Noelle said. "But when family problems arise, we are united."

Susannah felt her heart sink. What did that mean?

"So you are together?" another called.

"Let's go, Noelle," Jared almost growled.

"What about Susannah Chapman? Where does she stand in this?" another asked.

Susannah wanted to sink through the floor. She should never have come. Or at the very least should have thought of a disguise. How would she get out of here undetected?

"We are both anxious to help her move on in her life. It was unfortunate things turned out as they did," Noelle said.

Susannah waited for Jared to speak. The throng moved down the hall toward the elevators. Suddenly, the confusion eased and the hallway was once more quiet as people went about their business.

She peeped around the column toward the elevators. Noelle still clung to Jared's arm, smiling at reporters. He looked angry, but maintained silence.

Susannah looked for the sign for the stairs and headed there. She'd take them to the lobby and slip out without anyone knowing she'd been here.

At least today had given her an idea of what to expect during the trial. She'd ask Steve Johnson to provide some sort of security for her when she had to testify. She didn't think she could run the gauntlet of reporters half as well as Noelle and Jared had.

All the way home she heard Noelle's words echo—when trouble came they were united.

Did that mean Susannah had been right? Jared hadn't wanted Noelle to see them together. She might jump to the wrong conclusions.

As Susannah had?

For a short time she'd truly believed she and Jared might have something special that could grow into love.

She leaned her head against the bus window and almost moaned aloud. Who was she kidding? Her feelings had grown into love. She'd kept the thoughts at bay until she had felt more certain. But they were there.

Only, she didn't think Jared felt the same way.

Everything lately pointed to his only spending time with her to assuage his guilt.

Had making love been his way to make up for years of a barren existence? She frowned. She couldn't bear that thought.

Surely there had to be some feelings on his part.

Maybe she'd misread the scene with Noelle. She knew she wanted Jared, that much was clear. But if they were giving their relationship a chance to work, why was he spending time with her?

It was still early afternoon when Susannah reached her apartment. She changed and went for a walk. The weather was blustery, snow forecast for that evening. But she didn't mind. It was exhilarating to be in the midst of the wind. She was warmly dressed. Even if she hadn't been, she'd take the tempest over the small apartment.

Walking until she was exhausted, she finally turned for home. She had some serious thinking to do, but every time she tried to concentrate, a picture of Molly floated in front of her. She would always cherish Saturday's meeting. Who knew, maybe in another ten or eleven years, Molly would come looking for her birth mother.

"And where will I be then?" she asked aloud. There was nothing holding her to Denver.

Making plans and thinking of places to live didn't take away the achy feeling she had about Jared. She'd only loved two men in her life, Shawn and Jared. One was taken away from her by Timothy Winters. The second because of his cousin Noelle.

Fate played unkind tricks.

SHE WAS HUNGRY when she returned to the apartment. She'd throw together something and eat in front of the television. It sounded lonely. She remembered how she and Shawn would talk away the dinner hour, sometimes not even noticing what they ate, they were so caught up in what the other had done during the day.

To her surprise, the message light was blinking on the answering machine. She had not had a message since she arrived. Was it a friend of Christine who didn't know she had gone home to convalesce? She pressed the button, and heard Jared's message asking her to call.

A second message from Jared followed. He said Timothy had been arraigned and bound over for trial, call him.

She ignored his summons and went to fix dinner. She had nothing to say to him.

When the phone rang, Susannah knew it was Jared.

"I've been trying to reach you," he said without preamble.

"I just got home."

"Timothy was arraigned today."

"I know, I was there."

"I didn't see you."

She knew that. He'd had eyes only for Noelle.

"I saw you with Noelle, then ducked out so the reporters wouldn't get me. I hadn't thought about them being there. Or Noelle."

"She was there to show support for her family. Her mother and father will return in time for the trial. It's a bad business."

"Excuse me if I don't have the same feelings about the matter. I've got to go." She hung up and turned back to the kitchenette. Her soup was warming. She didn't want to think about—

The phone rang again. This time Susannah let it ring, listening impassively to Jared's voice on the answering machine demanding she pick up.

"You're not the boss of me," she murmured, toasting cheese on bread beneath the broiler. Comfort food, she thought. After dinner, maybe she'd go back out and find an ice-cream place and have a double hot-fudge sundae.

He called three more times while she was eating. Susannah gave him credit for tenacity, if nothing else. Once she finished eating, she headed out for ice cream.

A half hour later, Susannah sat in the bustling creamery, idly watching the families around her as she savored her sundae. She felt lonely again. Maybe she should have called Eva to see if she wanted to indulge. But her friend was probably planning more bar hopping and was surely more interested in interviewing the future Mr. Eva than in hearing Susannah's tale of woe.

Being alone in the midst of all these happy families once again reminded her of all she'd lost. Her anger against Timothy and Michael and even Jared rose again. Seeing justice served would help mitigate the feeling of being in a shadow world. Maybe one day she'd resolve things, but for now, she clung to the anger. It eased the hurt that would overwhelm her if she let it get a toehold.

JARED WAS FURIOUS. First Noelle, then Susannah. What was it with those women? He'd made a mistake going with Noelle to the hearing that morning. She'd turned the entire event into a circus.

Now Susannah didn't answer the blasted phone. He leaned back and stared at the ceiling. Had she heard Noelle's innuendoes this morning and thought the worst?

He didn't believe she ever trusted him. She saw him as one of the prosecution team from eight years ago. Was she merely taking what help he offered as her due? Had she ever seen him apart from the situation? Seen him for the man he was.

A man trying to atone for a grievous wrong.

He listened to the words echo in his mind. She couldn't think that was all there was to their relationship. He'd put his job on the line for her. Bent a hundred rules, or laws, to find out about her daughter. Did she think it was all some elaborate plan to make up for things?

Was she just hanging in for the ride? To see how much he'd offer until the well ran dry? Then what? She'd spoken about moving somewhere away from Denver.

Didn't she realize he wanted her, with all the longing in his heart. He loved her. What would he have to do to prove that?

He could only tell her and hope she believed him. Hope she felt the same, or would one day. Could she love him? Was her heart lost to Shawn forever?

She was still young, had an entire lifetime ahead of her. She liked Eric, there was no denying that. If they married, they could have children together. Not to make up for the loss of her first daughter, but to give her the family she so longed for. That he had once thought to have.

Marriage.

Jared drew in a deep breath. After his marriage to Noelle, he'd sworn not to get involved. Maybe he wasn't husband material.

But Susannah made him want to try again. Yearn to try again—with her. To see her in the morning over breakfast. To snuggle with her in bed at night. Go for long walks, help her each time she experienced that claustrophobia. Fill her days with happiness.

She was touchy, prickly, defensive, and he couldn't blame her after what had happened. But she had to know a bright future awaited. He just hoped she'd let it include him.

Marriage. The thought scared him. Yet at the same time, he felt exhilarated. He wanted her. Not just for a night or two, but forever.

Tomorrow he'd look for a ring. Call her for a dinner date. He'd take her to the Brown Hotel, the fanciest place he knew. After a romantic meal, he'd ask her to marry him.

She'd say yes. He hoped.

NOELLE PACED the living room. She had been waiting for Jared's call all evening. She'd told him when he put her into that cab after the arraignment to call her. Why hadn't he?

She turned and stalked back the way she'd come. Dammit, he had to know she'd be waiting to hear from him. They had to plan strategy with the mess Timothy had plunged the family into. Jared would want to protect his son. And his own livelihood. One reporter asked about the earlier trial today, but Jared had given him his standard no comment reply.

She was annoyed with Timothy for causing the situation, but maybe it would work to her advantage. If she could just get Jared to see she'd changed. They were so good together, it was time they reunited.

She thought her comments at the courthouse had been well timed. A few more and he'd have to see they were meant to be together.

But he needed to get over his white-knight complex where that woman was concerned. Sure, she'd received a raw deal. But it was hardly Jared's fault. Michael Denning had been the district attorney. The jury had found her guilty, not Jared. He'd done more than enough to make things up to Susannah Chapman. She was undoubtedly trying to get all she could from the man. Had she no conscience?

Jared should be with his son. She'd have to make him see that. After what he'd done for that woman, it was time to call a halt before she tricked him into more. Maybe a word in Steve Johnson's ear would turn the tide. It might be risky, she didn't know Johnson that well. But anything was worth a risk to have Jared back.

The phone rang.

Jared at last. She considered letting it ring to show him how it felt to feel ignored. But she'd waited too long for that.

"Hello?" She'd keep it light. He hated scenes.

"Noelle?" Martin said.

"Martin, how lovely to hear your voice." She glanced at the clock. "Isn't it a bit late there?"

"I'm in Denver. I'll be here a few days, packing things up, arranging to lease out my place. Would you care to have dinner with me tomorrow night?"

"I have plans. I wish I had known you were coming into town." Would he hear about her claims to the reporters? What if Jared didn't call? She couldn't afford to alienate Martin.

"I'm disappointed, though not surprised. You're a popular lady. Any other evening free?"

She had tomorrow free, had been hoping Jared would ask her out for dinner, or ask to come to dinner here to see Eric. It wasn't that late, he could still call.

"I'm free Thursday, if that would work with you."

"I'll look forward to it. We have some things to discuss."

She clenched the receiver, wishing he'd waited another week or two to return to Denver. This was too crucial a juncture with Jared to deal with Martin.

"I'll see you then," she said, and hung up.

He was going to ask her to marry him once again, she just knew it. Wandering to the fireplace, she studied her reflection in the huge mirror over the mantel. Why couldn't she want the man who wanted her? Why was she so hung up on Jared?

Because he'd left her? He'd been so devoted when they were first married. She hadn't changed—he had.

If she'd been the one to end their marriage, would she still want him back? Noelle paused a moment, struck by the idea.

SUSANNAH WAS SURPRISED when Jared called her at work the next morning. Obviously not wanting to leave any more fruitless messages on her machine, he'd gone through her boss.

"Hello?"

"I wanted to invite you to dinner," Jared said.

"I'm busy." She glanced at Pete, trying not to let the irritation she felt show.

"I didn't say when."

"Doesn't matter."

"Friday evening? I have something I want to discuss with you."

Thankfully Pete left the office, heading out to the loading dock.

Susannah turned her back to the door. "I'm busy Friday, and every other night between now and the end of time. Thank you for all you've done for me. I appreciate the job. And the apartment. I'm already looking so I'll have a place when Christine returns.

And thank you for finding my daughter and letting me see her. I'll always remember your kindness in that. But I don't see any need to keep in touch. I have my life, you have yours.''

"What's going on, Susannah?"

"Nothing's going on. You offered help, I accepted. I don't need anything more. Consider any debt paid in full."

"I didn't help you out because I felt it a debt."

She heard the frustration in his voice.

"Yes, you did."

He was silent for a moment.

"Maybe at first, but only at first," he said.

"Whatever. I have to go, I'm at work."

"So am I. Go to dinner with me so we can discuss this."

"There's nothing further to discuss. Thank you again for all you've done." She hung up the phone and took a deep breath.

It didn't help. She thought she'd feel better bringing things to an end. But she didn't. It hurt. All of it hurt.

"You okay?" Eva asked when Susannah rejoined her at the workbench.

"No, but I will be. I just had to tie up some loose ends."

"So, want to go with me on Friday night? There's a new place that's supposed to be hot. Live music. Live guys."

Susannah didn't hesitate. Time to move on. "I'd love to."

CHAPTER SIXTEEN

SUSANNAH TRIMMED the branches of a tree, making sure it was as perfect as possible. It had been two weeks since she'd last spoken with Jared. Winter was taking hold. The days were short. The nights too long for the thoughts that wouldn't give her peace.

The Christmas tree section of the nursery was bustling, while the rest of the business was quiet.

She missed Jared. Missed knowing what he was doing. She missed being with him and Eric.

Both were dear to her and she wondered if they even thought about her.

She'd gone out with Eva four times so far, and each time had been a lesson in tedium. She didn't like the loud music, didn't like the groping hands of the men they met. And she didn't like the effects of liquor. If Timothy hadn't been drunk when he crashed his car with Shawn as a passenger, none of her past eight years would have happened.

She'd given it a fair try. The next time Eva asked, she'd refuse.

Restless, she glanced around for the next project. Pete was cutting back hours now that most of the work for the year was winding up. There'd be little to do until spring came.

She was lucky he didn't let her go. She'd been last hired, and knew it had been a favor to Jared. She worked hard to justify Jared's belief in her, as well as Pete's.

Today she was leaving at noon. That would set the pattern for the next several weeks. Half days. Some worked mornings, some afternoons. She'd chosen mornings. With the extra time, she planned to walk home. Each day she'd choose a different route to see if there were apartments she might like to rent before Christine returned.

During the long nights, when she couldn't sleep, she'd made a list of things to do. She'd passed her driver's test last week, using Eva's car. She was far from being able to afford a vehicle of her own, but having the license meant she finally had identification, and she fit in.

She'd opened a checking account and a savings account and banked most of her paycheck. She knew she'd have to pay a hefty deposit to rent a place.

She'd started a journal for her daughter. Writing how she thought about things, and how she had wanted more than she'd been given, she poured her feelings out. If Molly ever came looking for her, she wanted her to know that Susannah had loved her always. And if she never came, at least Susannah knew she was keeping her daughter in her life, if only through the words on the pages.

Tomorrow, Susannah would pay her weekly visit to the library. In an effort to keep herself from thinking about Jared, she'd checked out a few cookbooks and tried her hand at baking and cooking. The successes she took to work and shared. The failures, few though they were, she dumped in the trash, only Cocoa knowing.

When she found a recipe she liked, she copied it on index cards, and already had quite a few. She liked cooking. If she didn't have this unreasonable fear of being confined, she could look for work as a cook somewhere if Pete ended up letting her go.

Or maybe she should look at working on a ranch. There were plenty of them in Colorado. She had no experience, but could learn. She'd have to pick up some books on ranching and see if she could get an idea about a job she could handle.

By the time she reached home, it was windy and threatening rain. She walked up the sidewalk and turned toward the lobby of the building then stopped. Noelle Walker was standing just inside the double glass doors.

Great, just what she needed.

She pushed open the doors.

"Hello," Noelle said. She looked stunning, as always, in her designer suit and fashionable winter coat.

"What do you want?" Susannah was past being polite to this woman. Hadn't she done enough?

"I wanted to speak with you, if you can spare the

time.'' Noelle looked over Susannah from head to toe, her thoughts obvious.

''I don't think we have anything to say to one another,'' Susannah said.

''No, I don't suppose you do. But Martin said I should try. I'm leaving tomorrow for London.''

''Who's Martin?''

Noelle raised an eyebrow. ''Ah, so something piques your curiosity. I called at the nursery and was told you'd already left for the day. Invite me upstairs and I'll tell you why I'm here.''

Susannah debated. No matter what, she came off the worse in any confrontation with Noelle Walker. Still, she was curious as to why Noelle would seek her out. Didn't she have all she wanted?

''If you aren't staying long, come on up,'' Susannah said, moving to the elevator.

''If I were staying longer, I'd offer you some lessons in manners,'' Noelle snapped, following her.

Her perfume filled the lobby. Susannah resented it. Resented her perfect hair, her lovely clothes, her air of superiority and her claim to Jared.

Stepping into the elevator, Susannah turned to watch her unexpected guest. Noelle reached up to brush a strand of hair back, the glint of a diamond ring almost blinding Susannah.

The ring was on Noelle's left hand.

Susannah felt sick. Suddenly she didn't care a bit about Noelle or what she had to say. London was probably a honeymoon trip with Jared. Had the woman come only to gloat? Susannah would not give her the pleasure of showing any emotion. Let her think she didn't care.

Cocoa came running when Susannah opened the door. He wound himself around her legs as she bent over to pat him. Noelle sidestepped around the cat, taking in the student furnishing of Christine's apartment.

"Cozy," she said, moving to sit on the edge of the old sofa.

Susannah shrugged out of her jacket and tossed it on a chair. She sat in another one. "Say what you came to say, then leave."

Noelle closed her eyes for a moment, then opened them. "I will never understand it."

"What?"

"What Jared sees in you."

"Guilt," Susannah answered quickly enough.

"I don't think so. Anyway, Martin said I should come, so I did."

"And Martin is?"

"My fiancé," Noelle said, waving her left hand in front of Susannah's face.

"Fiancé? What about Jared?"

"Yes, well, I tried. I still don't understand it, and I'm not sure I ever will. And if you ever tell a soul, I'll deny it with my dying breath. I wanted him. He wants you."

Susannah looked at her in stunned disbelief.

Noelle nodded, obviously vexed. "I thought for

sure he'd stand by us when Timothy was brought in. But he just says let the chips fall where they may. Enough harm has been done because of Timothy."

"He feels guilty because of my wrongful conviction," Susannah said.

"I wish that was all of it. But there's more. Anyway, Martin said I should clear the air and make sure you knew the field was open, so to speak. We're leaving in the morning."

"For London."

"Yes. Martin's business has posted him there for an indefinite period. I'm sure I'll love it. And we'll be so close to Paris and Amsterdam. I'm looking forward to quick weekend visits."

"You're taking Eric?"

"No." For a moment, Noelle looked stricken. "No, Eric is staying with Jared. I'll miss him, but he's started school, and has his playmates. Jared loves him."

"Of course he does. Eric's a great little boy."

Noelle nodded. "I think so, too. Though a handful sometimes. It's always surprised me how much Jared wants to be with him, after his own father's behavior."

"What behavior?"

"The man was a drunken bum who couldn't hold a job longer than two weeks and didn't like to see his son do well. Showed him up, even when Jared was younger. I don't think he ever had a fatherly feeling in his life."

Susannah remembered their dinner, when Jared had spoken about his father.

"I like to think I had some influence on grooming him to be the man he is today," Noelle said.

"I expect he did it all himself," Susannah retorted. She felt as if the world was shifting on its axis. "Exactly why are you here?" she asked Noelle.

"I'm giving you Jared and Eric," she said.

"They aren't yours to give."

"Well, I'm letting you know you have my blessing, then," Noelle said, clearly annoyed. "I thought you'd knock me down in your hurry to go see him."

"Jared was only helping me because of guilt. All obligations to me were cleared when he found my daughter. There's nothing else between us. I haven't seen him in weeks."

Noelle picked up on the first part. "He found your daughter?"

Susannah didn't want to talk to Noelle. She wished she'd never let her in the apartment.

"I told you before, I was pregnant when I was sent to prison. I gave my baby up for adoption."

"And Jared found her. How extraordinary. Mr. Law-and-Order broke the law to find an adopted child?"

"He didn't break any laws," Susannah said.

"Oh, no? Colorado has sealed adoptions. People can't just waltz in and find an adopted child."

Susannah didn't say anything. She knew it wouldn't have been easy, but she didn't like thinking he'd violated his sense of what was right to find her child for her.

"That explains Jared. Now it's all up to you," Noelle said, rising. "I'll see myself out." She reached into her purse and pulled out a folded sheet of paper. She held it out to Susannah.

"I didn't think you'd remember the way, so I wrote the directions for you. It's to Jared's place in the mountains. Go and see for yourself."

"See what?" She took the paper and stood.

"See if it's guilt or something more." Noelle sauntered to the door.

With that cryptic comment, she left.

SUSANNAH DEBATED with herself all the rest of the afternoon and evening. The next morning she was no closer to a decision than she'd been when Noelle had given her the paper.

Should she go out to the cabin? What would she find there? Eric and Jared, if Noelle was to be believed.

But to what end?

So Jared and Noelle weren't back together. Susannah was still baffled by the sudden change of events. She'd thought for sure Noelle wanted Jared. Now she was engaged to someone else?

Not that it meant Jared wanted *her*. He'd been kind. That was all.

It had been more than two weeks since she'd heard

from him. She ached to see him. Longed to have him kiss her, hold her.

Still, she couldn't convince herself that what they'd shared was enough to base a lifetime commitment upon. How could she know he wanted her, that he wasn't just trying to make up for things. What would convince her?

Nothing.

He could say it a hundred times, but he could be lying. How would she ever know?

"YOU'VE BEEN awfully quiet this morning," Eva commented as their shift ended. The shorter workdays gave them extra time on the weekends. Eva had extended her usual invitation to bar hop, which Susannah had turned down.

"Anything wrong?"

"I'm not sure. Not wrong, exactly. But puzzling."

"Tell me, I'm great at coming up with answers to puzzling situations. I'm more street-smart than you, and have been around the block," Eva said.

"Noelle Walker came to see me yesterday and suggested I go see Jared this weekend," Susannah said slowly.

"Whoa, hold the phone. What did you say? I thought they were getting back together."

"I thought so, too, from what I saw at the courthouse a few weeks ago. But she's engaged to someone named Martin. She even gave me directions to Jared's home."

"Why?"

"I haven't a clue. Do you think it's some kind of trick? Something that'll make me look like a complete idiot and have her coming out like some superhero?" Susannah asked.

"Not from what you've told me about her, or what I've seen. Nothing can make her look like a superhero."

Susannah smiled. Her bias toward Noelle had been conveyed to her friend. Still, did she owe it to herself to go and see what Jared had to say?

"So go," Eva said. "What can it hurt?"

"What can it help?"

"I don't know. Maybe she thinks if you see him again you'll fall in a puddle at his feet."

"Everything he's done for me has been because of what happened," Susannah said.

"Do you know that for a fact?"

"How could it be anything else? He didn't know me at the beginning."

"People change."

"How would I ever know?"

"Some things you have to take on faith," Eva said. "Want to borrow my car?"

Susannah was tempted. Was she hoping for a miracle? Hoping somehow Jared would convince her he loved her.

"No. Thanks anyway."

"Let me know if you change your mind. Sure you

don't want to come with me tonight? There's a new spot—''

"And it's really hot, and so are the guys," Susannah finished for her.

They laughed. But Susannah felt sorry for Eva. She wanted so much to be part of a couple. As did she. Was it that longing that made her see things that didn't exist?

She began her long walk home, the yearning to see Jared growing with each step. Was he really not involved with Noelle?

She touched the paper folded in her pocket. She could drive out and see. She didn't even have to speak to him, just park off somewhere and watch when he and Eric arrived.

She'd do it.

She caught the next bus, no longer content with the time it would take to walk home. Once at the apartment, she called Eva.

"I've changed my mind," she said when Eva picked up.

"You'll go with me?"

"No. I want to borrow your car."

SUSANNAH FOLLOWED the directions carefully. Gripping the steering wheel, she kept to the right lane on the highway, letting all the other drivers pass her. It had been too long since she'd driven to be complacent.

Turning on the road that led to Jared's house, she

checked the directions again. Nothing looked familiar. Was it because of the snow? Trees and more trees swayed in the wind. Few homes and fewer cars. She wanted to get out and walk, but settled for opening the windows and letting the cold air blow through.

When she arrived at the driveway, she hesitated. She'd come all this way, might as well turn in.

Jared's car was not in sight, unless it was hidden behind all the other vehicles crowding in front of the house. Three pickup trucks and a panel van were parked haphazardly on dirty, slushy snow. Men were working, some on the deck, others around the side of the house.

Had there been a fire? The front wall was gone. Support beams held up the roof, while men framed in the space. She stopped behind the van and watched for a moment, trying to figure out what was going on. It was the middle of winter, no one would be doing construction without a good reason.

Finally she climbed out of the car and headed for the house.

"Excuse me," she said to one man wearing a hard hat and carrying a long roll of papers.

"What can I do for you?" he asked.

"What happened?" she asked, gesturing toward the house.

"Got to clear away the old to build the new," he said, tapping the roll against his thigh.

"Was there a fire?"

"No."

"Then what…" She stared at the mess.

"Owner wanted some changes and wasn't going to wait until spring to get them."

"What kind of changes?"

"Windows."

"Windows?"

"Floor-to-ceiling in almost every room, and a door to the outdoors in every room. Crazy if you ask me. Do you know how much it'll cost to heat this place with so much glass? But, hey, if he wants to spend his money doing it, fine by me. Winter is usually a slow time for us. We're glad for the job."

Floor-to-ceiling windows. Doors to the outside from every room. Susannah stared at the house as the words echoed in her mind.

Tears blurred her vision.

He'd done it for her.

This was the proof she wanted. The proof she needed to know he cared for *her*. No man would make such a gesture just to atone. Especially when he had every reason to believe he wouldn't see her again after their last conversation.

She stepped aside as two of the men carried a large double-pane window from the van and fit it into place.

Noelle had been right. She needed to be here today.

Stepping past them, she went inside. It was as cold inside as it was outside with no windows. She knew they wouldn't finish tonight. If Jared was coming, he and Eric were only going to check on things. Not stay. Not unless they planned to freeze to death.

She went in to the back and studied the changes in the kitchen, then to the bedrooms. True to the man's word, every outside wall had been gutted. Eric's room was finished. The windows needed to be cleaned, but the floor-to-ceiling panes and the new door were in. She stepped to the glass, feeling as if she were right in the heart of the woods.

Her heart sped up. She knew without being told, Jared had done this for her. Because he thought she'd be coming here often and wanted her to feel more comfortable.

No one had ever given her such a gift. How had he felt when she'd refused to see him, hadn't answered his phone calls? He'd done all this for her, and she'd turned her back on him.

Yet he had proceeded with the renovation.

"Ma'am, you shouldn't be in here." The construction worker she'd spoken with stood in the doorway.

"He did it for me," she said turning.

"Ma'am?"

"Never mind. I'll wait outside. Jared's coming here this afternoon?"

"So he said. You meeting him here?"

"Yes." Susannah walked back through the house, shivering a little in the cold. She was glad she'd worn warm clothes.

She went to the corner of the deck with the least amount of activity and leaned against the railing, watching the construction workers go about their tasks.

She was just beginning to wonder if she was going to have to go sit in Eva's car to prevent frostbite when she heard another vehicle on the driveway.

She watched as Jared drove in slowly and parked beyond her car. He hadn't seen her.

Suddenly she felt shy, awkward. She should have let him know she was coming. Or at the very least, should have called to apologize for not responding to his messages.

Now she'd have to apologize face-to-face.

Jared unfastened Eric's seat belt and helped the little boy from the car. She couldn't hear him, but she knew he was admonishing Eric to stay close to him and out of the way of the workers. It's what parents everywhere would have said.

They started toward the house. Eric spotted her first.

"Look, Daddy, it's Susannah!" With a whoop, he began to run directly to her.

Jared looked up, his step slowing.

Susannah hardly had time for a brief smile before Eric launched himself against her. She caught him in a tight hug.

"I've missed you," she said softly, holding him close for too brief a second. Then she released him and smiled at his beaming face.

"I haven't seen you in a long time. What have you been doing?" Eric asked. "Did you see the changes Daddy made for you? Do you like our house now?"

"I did see and I do like it. I liked it before."

"Yes, but you gots scared being closed inside. Now you can pretend you're in the woods all the time."

Jared climbed onto the deck, ignoring the workers, focused solely on Susannah.

She smiled tentatively.

"I think I have issues with trust," she said.

"I can understand that."

She waved her hand. "Did you do all this for me?"

He nodded.

"We haven't even spoken in weeks."

"Doesn't change the fact I want you in my life."

Her heart rate sped up. She studied his face, seeing the sincerity there. And something more. Dare she hope?

"I thought you and Noelle were getting back together."

"Mommy went to London," Eric interjected.

Jared looked at him. "She did. Why don't you walk by the workers—carefully—and go see how your room turned out."

"Okay." He started to turn, then looked at Susannah. "Are you spending the weekend with us? We get to camp out 'cause we don't have all the windows in yet."

"You're going to camp out in this weather?" It was close to freezing in the sunny afternoon—how much colder would it get in the middle of the night?

"We are. We're tough," Jared said, teasing her. "Want to stay?"

"More than anything," she said softly, forgetting the cold, the strangers who swarmed around them, the little boy standing so close by, watching every gesture.

"I'll keep you warm," Jared said.

"All night long?" she teased.

"All life long, if you'll let me," he replied.

Her breath caught.

"Eric, Susannah is staying. Go check out your room. Be careful around the workmen."

"I want Susannah to see it," he said.

"She will. Go on, we'll be there in a minute."

He waited until Eric was safely in the house, then took Susannah's arm and drew her down the steps and away from the commotion surrounding the renovations.

They walked down the drive, out of earshot, but still in visual distance in case Eric came back outside.

"I planned a romantic dinner, maybe dancing. Time to talk, to sort things out. Then I wanted to ask you to marry me," he said when they stopped.

"Marry you?"

"Will you?" He reached into his jacket pocket and pulled out a small jeweler's box. Opening it, he showed her a beautiful diamond ring in a simple setting. "I've been carrying this around for two weeks."

She stared at it, then raised her gaze to his. "Why?"

"Why?"

"Why marriage? Why me?"

He snapped the box shut and put it back in his pocket. "Why do people usually marry?" he said testily.

"For many reasons, actually. I want to know yours."

He glanced around, then looked back at her. "Because I love you."

Susannah's heart melted. "You don't look so happy about it."

"A man would like some assurance the woman he wants to marry might feel warmly enough toward him to give him some confidence when he tells her he loves her. But I get hung up on, no return calls. Talk about an ego buster."

"It's not guilt then?" she asked.

"Susannah, I'm sorry as hell that you were wrongfully convicted. I sat at the prosecution table, but I was too new to do anything but learn. Blame the system, the blind ambition of Michael Denning or whatever. I'd change the past if I could, but I know now that what happened to you was not my fault. For what it's worth, you can trust me to keep you safe as long as I live. I'm no longer some green-as-grass lawyer starting out. You can trust me to take care of you."

"And love me?"

"As long as I live."

It was enough, more than enough—it was everything.

She flung herself against him, feeling his strong arms come around to hold her tightly, despite the thick bulky clothes. "I love you, Jared Walker. I'd be so happy to be your wife."

He kissed her. They broke away when they heard the cheers from the workers. Susannah blushed and hid her face against Jared's shoulder.

"Good grief, an audience."

"They're happy for us," he said, rubbing his hand over her back. "But I'll be glad when they finish for the day and leave. There's one thing I should mention," he said.

"What?" She pulled back.

"Eric comes with the deal."

"Well, of course he does, he's your son. I love him as much as I do Molly. I'm glad he'll be a part of the deal."

"Full-time. Noelle agreed to joint custody, then took off for London indefinitely. I'll have Eric full-time for the next few years."

"She came by to see me yesterday."

"What?"

"How do you think I came here today? She almost ordered me here, and gave me directions."

"I will never understand that woman."

"I thought the two of you were getting back together," Susannah said.

"No."

"I saw you both at the arraignment. I heard her comments to the press."

"She was making a last-ditch effort to get me back. But I told her it would never happen, and why. How could I even think of her when all I could think about was you?''

"She's beautiful, comes from a fine family. She could even help you professionally.'' Susannah didn't know why she kept harping on Noelle, maybe to hear him deny all the fears that were in her heart.

He held her shoulders, looking deep into her eyes. ''You are beautiful. Your family is fine with me and I don't need any help professionally, I can handle that myself. You are who I want to share my life with. You make me forget my fears about commitment. I never planned to marry again, but being with you changed my mind. I know you have trust issues. I probably have a few myself. But together, don't you think we can conquer anything?''

"Yes.'' She reached up for a quick kiss, then brushed her fingertips over his cheeks. "I love you, Jared Walker, and I always will.''

"Then let's go home.'' He tucked her hand in the crook of his arm and they walked back to the house that would truly become their home.

EPILOGUE

Eight years later

"ERIC, HURRY UP, we're ready to leave," Jared called to his older son. The two younger children were ready to go sledding. Only their teenaged son was holding them up.

"Mommy, I haf to go potty," three-year-old Joshua said.

"Oh, Josh, I just got your snowsuit zipped," Susannah complained. She looked at Jared. "Your turn. I can't bend over as much as I normally can."

Six months pregnant with their third child, Susannah was moving more carefully these days. She had cut back at the Christmas tree farm she'd started across the highway from their home on some of the acreage Jared had bought. And her own garden shop was in hiatus until spring. After the baby came.

Susannah still had moments when she remembered the horrors of her past. But knowing Timothy was incarcerated for life with no possibility of parole made her feel that justice had been done. And the moments were fewer each year. Being with Jared made all the difference. Her heart was full, and there was little room for regrets over what couldn't be changed.

"I'll take care of him. Why don't you take Marissa outside before she gets too hot. We'll join you as soon as I get Eric going and Josh ready," Jared said, holding out his hand for his younger son.

"We're never going to get out of here," she said, laughing. It always took longer than she expected to get everyone mobilized. She should be used to it.

"You don't need to be so impatient, you're not going to sled, just supervise," Jared said.

"I know. I'll have to wait until next year to have any fun."

"I don't know about fun, just sledding," he said suggestively, brushing back her hair and kissing her cheek.

The phone rang.

"I'll get that, you get Josh to the bathroom. Marissa, honey, Mommy will just be a minute, okay? Wait on the deck for me."

"Okay." The five-year-old named for Susannah's best friend went out to the deck and was soon making snowballs to pelt at her older brother. Eric teased her all the time, but she stood up for herself, and was getting prepared early this time.

Susannah answered the phone.

"Is this Susannah Walker?"

"Yes."

"My name is Molly Bradley. My mom said you would be expecting my call one day."

"Molly." Susannah's knees went weak. She sank into the chair near the phone. "Yes, I mean, I was hoping you'd call sometime. How are you?"

"My mom said you're my biological mother. She told me what happened. Is it all right if we meet sometime?"

"I'd love it. Whenever you say. Want to come out to the house today? We're going sledding, but we can wait until you get here, if you like. Or go back out."

It was Molly, her daughter. She gripped the receiver tightly and heard her laugh.

"I haven't been sledding in a long time."

"Come today, then. And your parents."

"It's weird, isn't it? I mean Mom and Dad are my parents, but you are, too. I read your letter."

Susannah bit back tears. "I'm so glad you want to meet me, I've missed you all your life."

"Let me ask my parents if we can come. Then you can tell my mother where you live."

A moment later Rebecca Bradley came on the line.

"Hello, Susannah. I know you've waited for this call for a long time."

"Rebecca, thank you."

"Hey, she's a great kid. You'll love her as much as we do. You really want us all to descend on you on such short notice?"

"Oh, yes. I can't wait to see her again. Thank you for the photographs over the years, and the notes. They've meant so much."

"We appreciate that you kept your word, that you

didn't try to see her, or take her away from us. She's still our delight.''

"I know what you mean. I now have three children of my own and another on the way.''

"Give me the directions and we'll be out this afternoon.''

When she hung up the phone, Jared and Josh came down the hall, trailed by Eric.

"Who called?'' Jared asked.

"Molly,'' Susannah said, still stunned by the news. Today she'd see her daughter for the third time. And this time Molly knew who she was and wanted to meet her.

"Your daughter?''

She nodded, smiling through her tears. "I can't believe it.''

Jared took her in his arms and hugged her. "This calls for a celebration.''

"They're coming out this afternoon. I said we'd go sledding again.''

"Yippee, we gets to go two times today,'' Josh said jumping around.

"Cool, Mom. But she's not going to boss me around, is she, just because she's a couple of years older?'' Eric asked. At thirteen, and as tall as Susannah, he enjoyed being the older brother. He saw his mother each year when she flew in to Denver for a visit, although he had yet to show any interest in going to London to visit Noelle. Susannah was grateful for the love he'd given her.

As she was for all her children. And Jared.

He had made it all possible. Their love had grown stronger as the years passed by. Their family had flourished in happiness and love. And today it would be complete. She'd hold her firstborn in her arms at long last.

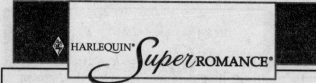

HARLEQUIN *Super*ROMANCE®

A Family Christmas
by Carrie Alexander

(Harlequin Superromance #1239)

All Rose Robbin ever wanted was a family
Christmas—just like the ones she'd seen on TV—but
being a Robbin (one of those Robbins) pretty much
guaranteed she'd never get one. Especially after
circumstances had her living "down" to
everyone else's expectations.

After a long absence, Rose is back in Alouette,
primarily to help out her impossible-to-please mother,
but also to keep tabs on the child she wasn't allowed
to keep. Working hard, helping her mother and trying
to steal glimpses of her child seem to be all that's in
Wild Rose's future—until the day single father
Evan Grant catches her in the act.

NORTH COUNTRY
Stories

Alouette, Michigan.
Located high on the Upper
Peninsula—home to strong
men, stalwart women and
lots and lots of trees.

Available in November 2004 *wherever Harlequin books are sold*

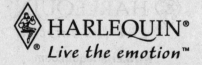

HARLEQUIN®
Live the emotion™

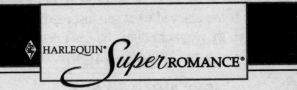

Seattle after Midnight
by C.J. Carmichael

(Superromance #1240)

On sale November 2004

"Hello, Seattle. Welcome to 'Georgia after
Midnight,' the show for lonely hearts
and lovers...."

P.I. Pierce Harding can't resist listening to
Georgia Lamont's late-night radio show.
Something about her sultry voice calls to him.
But Georgia has also attracted an unwanted
listener, one who crosses the line between fan
and fanatic. When the danger escalates,
Pierce knows that he will do anything to keep
Georgia safe. Even risk his heart...

Available wherever Harlequin books are sold

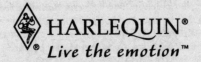

If you enjoyed what you just read,
then we've got an offer you can't resist!

Take 2 bestselling love stories FREE!
Plus get a FREE surprise gift!

Clip this page and mail it to Harlequin Reader Service®

IN U.S.A.
3010 Walden Ave.
P.O. Box 1867
Buffalo, N.Y. 14240-1867

IN CANADA
P.O. Box 609
Fort Erie, Ontario
L2A 5X3

YES! Please send me 2 free Harlequin Superromance® novels and my free surprise gift. After receiving them, if I don't wish to receive anymore, I can return the shipping statement marked cancel. If I don't cancel, I will receive 6 brand-new novels every month, before they're available in stores. In the U.S.A., bill me at the bargain price of $4.69 plus 25¢ shipping and handling per book and applicable sales tax, if any*. In Canada, bill me at the bargain price of $5.24 plus 25¢ shipping and handling per book and applicable taxes**. That's the complete price, and a savings of at least 10% off the cover prices—what a great deal! I understand that accepting the 2 free books and gift places me under no obligation ever to buy any books. I can always return a shipment and cancel at any time. Even if I never buy another book from Harlequin, the 2 free books and gift are mine to keep forever.

135 HDN DZ7W
336 HDN DZ7X

Name	(PLEASE PRINT)	
Address	Apt.#	
City	State/Prov.	Zip/Postal Code

Not valid to current Harlequin Superromance® subscribers.

Want to try two free books from another series?
Call 1-800-873-8635 or visit www.morefreebooks.com.

* Terms and prices subject to change without notice. Sales tax applicable in N.Y.
** Canadian residents will be charged applicable provincial taxes and GST.
    All orders subject to approval. Offer limited to one per household.
    ® are registered trademarks owned and used by the trademark owner and or its licensee.

SUP04R   ©2004 Harlequin Enterprises Limited

Christmas comes to

HARLEQUIN ROMANCE®

In November 2004, don't miss:

CHRISTMAS EVE MARRIAGE
(#3820)

by Jessica Hart

In this seasonal romance, the only thing Thea is
looking for on her long-awaited holiday is a little
R and R—she certainly doesn't expect to find herself
roped into being Rhys Kingsford's pretend fiancée!

A SURPRISE
CHRISTMAS PROPOSAL
(#3821)

by Liz Fielding

A much-needed job brings sassy Sophie Harrington up
close and personal with rugged bachelor Gabriel York
in this festive story. But how long before he realizes
that Sophie isn't just for Christmas—but for life...?

Available wherever Harlequin books are sold.

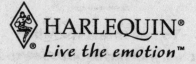

HARLEQUIN®
Live the emotion™

www.eHarlequin.com

HRCTJHLF